THE

OF HUMORC

ALDINE PAPERBACKS

THE TREASURY OF

Humorous Quotations

EDITED BY EVAN ESAR

ENGLISH EDITION

EDITED BY

Nicolas Bentley

J. M. DENT & SONS LTD

Made in Great Britain
by
Morrison & Gibb Ltd · London and Edinburgh
for
J. M. DENT & SONS LTD
Aldine House · Bedford Street · London
First published by Phoenix House Ltd 1951
Reprinted 1952
Third Impression 1952
First published in this edition 1962
Reprinted 1962, 1964, 1967, 1971

ISBN 0 460 02002 1

Foreword

I DON'T know why, but dictionaries of quotations and treasuries of humour generally ignore comic sayings. This became apparent to me in the course of my research for this book. I had encountered many comic sayings, but when I tried to check them in such reference books I found that most of them were omitted. So I decided to compile an anthology of witticisms, and here it is—a combination treasury of humour and dictionary of quotations. Because of its dual nature, this anthology supplements the excellent works in these fields. It does not pretend to compete with them.

After having collected thousands of comic items, my problem was to organize them for ready reference. I knew that quotation dictionaries are usually arranged according to subject, and treasuries of humour according to author. This collection, it seemed to me, belonged in structure to the latter type. So I put its contents in a frame of author reference. And to add to its usefulness I added a subject index.

When authors are listed with their own sayings grouped under them, their personalities become clear to us at once. We notice their individual styles, how they achieve their comic effects, and how their wit differs from that of others. We observe quickly and easily the sweet of Thoreau, the sour of Nietzsche, the salt of Samuel Butler, and the bitter of Bierce.

Sometimes authors reveal themselves by the subjects they choose. As Goethe learned from his own lack of humour: 'Men show their character in nothing more clearly than by what they find laughable'. But more often, it is by temperament rather than by subject that they reveal themselves. The wit of Swift is chiefly satire, but in Lamb it is word-play, in Hazlitt it is scepticism, and in Sydney Smith it is drollery.

Each of these styles has its own individual bias. Compare with Americans these Britons and note how their temperaments vary. The satire of Swift differs from the satire of Mencken, the word-play of Lamb from the word-play of Oliver Herford, the scepticism of Hazlitt from the scepticism of Robert Frost, and the drollery of Smith from the drollery of Don Herold.

Lord, what fools these immortals be,
But how immortal their foolery.

If brevity is the soul of wit, variety is the mark of it. You will find ample evidence of variety here—fun in the profundity of Anatole France, jests in the suggestions of Douglas Jerrold. You will even find wit in Whitman, and in other such humourless spirits who occasionally struck comic effects by accident. All types of comic quotations are included in this collection—nonsense, satire, caricature, paradoxes, wellerisms, reversibles.

This work is made up roughly of three parts: two centuries of English wit, one century of American wit, and the rest of a more ancient and foreign vintage. My emphasis on modern humour is easily understood. The older the wit, the less quotable. Many an excellent witticism of older writers like Shakespeare has been omitted because proverbial over-use has destroyed its original comic appeal. Benjamin Franklin's saying, for example, 'We must all hang together or we shall all hang separately', was once a great epigram; but it has long ceased to be funny and is remembered now only for its historic association. This illustrates an important distinction between comic and non-comic quotations. The former lose their piquancy by frequent repetition, whereas the latter acquire acceptance by it. Familiarity breeds serious quotations but buries comic ones.

There are other reasons why I have stressed modern humour in this collection. I shall not go into them here, for they would make dull reading. One point, though, is worth mentioning. The older literary wit was largely expressed in rigid verse patterns. Not until the eighteenth century did it finally shake off these shackles and become enormously more flexible. My desire to make this book as quotable as possible led me to omit verse, with the occasional exception of a couplet in prose form. This in turn meant the omission of much pre-eighteenth-century wit, which consisted largely of verse.

The inclusion of contemporaries presented several problems. Since more interest attaches to the remarks of a notability than to those of a nonentity, it is common practice in periodical literature to tag anonymous flashes of wit on to famous names. This applies particularly to radio and Hollywood comedians. Fortunately my familiarity with gag-file wit has enabled me to exclude most of these false credits. I have also excluded many apocryphal quotations customarily attached to wits like Oscar Wilde, malaprop-makers like Samuel Goldwyn, and columnists like 'Beachcomber', who give wide currency to comedy lines.

Another problem of handling the wit of contemporaries is the difficulty of doing justice to them. I cannot pretend even to have approximated justice. Nevertheless, I have included far more contemporary items than any other collection of quotations or of humour.

When I began this work I considered confining it to original English quotations, for translation is the sworn enemy of wit. *Traduttori, traditori* applies as much to the comic as to the poetic. But there was always Voltaire and a host of others whose salty sayings even in translation I would not willingly forgo. So I decided to include them. Of these, the French are the most numerous, for theirs has the wittiest tradition of all European tongues; and among them La Rochefoucauld excels, though he is less witty than wise. As for other foreigners, two individuals are worth passing notice here, for they underscore the translation limitations of wit and they deserve as many pages in this book as they are given lines. Heine, one of the wittiest of the moderns, seems to lose his sparkle when converted into English, and this is as true of his smiling prose as of his poetry. And Martial, one of the wittiest of the ancients, must not only battle against the barriers of verse and translation but two millennia as well—an impossible task.

Although I have tried to ensure the accuracy of the contents of this book, there may be a number of items which are not reproduced here perfectly. Misquotations of language persist because they are briefer or sharper or more rhythmic than their originals. For example, Shakespeare wrote: 'A young man married is a man that's marred'. But some unknown misquoter changed it to: 'A young man married is a young man marred', and that is the way it is usually expressed. I am tempted to misquote Emerson myself: 'Next to the originator of a good sentence is the first misquoter of it'.

The greater evil lies not with misquotations of language, as Byron thought, but with misquotations of source. Every epigrammatist finds some of his *bons mots* attributed to others, and naturally resents it. But fourth-century Donatus gave this matter an unexpected turn-about. 'Damn those', he exclaimed, 'who have made my remarks before me!' And in modern times that twist-wit Samuel Butler gave the idea of misquotation another twirl: 'It is bad enough', he said, 'to see one's own good things fathered on other people, but it is worse to have other people's rubbish fathered upon oneself'. Fortunate was Butler indeed to have lived before the age of columnists and digest-magazine fillers!

A point should be made here about identical quotations from different sources. Under the law of levity, as under the law of gravity, things tend to move toward each other. Thus we occasionally find famous men producing the same epigrams. For example, both Robert Ingersoll and Samuel Butler hit upon the identical reversible: 'An honest God is the noblest work of man'. I have generally avoided such duplication by entering only the quotation from the earlier source.

By the same token, much that is wittily expressed is unwittingly borrowed. Bill Nye said: 'Be virtuous and you will be happy, but you will be lonesome sometimes'. And Mark Twain said after him: 'Be good and you will be lonesome'. Nor is this the only instance where the greater unconsciously borrowed from the lesser wit, though more often it is the other way around. Dr Johnson said: 'If he does really think that there is no distinction between vice and virtue, when he leaves our houses let us count our spoons'. And Emerson said after him: 'The louder he talked of his honor, the faster we counted our spoons'. Such pairs of pared satire are inevitable in the nature of humour, and they occur more frequently than is realized. I have usually included such parallel items in this treasury.

Identity of idea rather than of language is, of course, another matter, and we need no Ecclesiastes come from the grave Old Testament to tell us that nothing is said that has not been said before. Certain subjects, like man and woman, husband

and wife, love and marriage, lend themselves eternally to caricature and ridicule. What wonder, then, that the same ideas are expressed by satirists of every generation! The same ideas, but every expression of them different. For example, to Wilde a gentleman was 'one who never hurts anyone's feelings unintentionally', whereas to Mencken he is 'one who never strikes a woman without provocation'.

Occasionally clever ideas are cleverly paraphrased. Such items have been included only when I thought the rewording sufficiently rewarding and not too close to the original. Thus you will find here Shakespeare's 'I am not only witty in myself but the cause that wit is in other men', as well as Johnson's 'He is not only dull himself but the cause of dullness in others'.

I have similarly included proverbial paraphrases, though these always follow the original closely because they are puns. For example, Addison Mizner's 'Absinthe makes the heart grow fonder', and 'Poets are born, not paid'. Most wits indulge in this type of word-play, and pun-loving Shakespeare was one of them. He revised the proverb 'Comparisons are odious' into 'Comparisons are odorous'—a pun that would be decried if uttered by a lesser wit. A number of proverb twisters will be found in this book—punsters like Ethel Watts Mumford who made an unwholesome hobby of it—but I have included only the best of their parodies.

I have taken the liberty of changing into orthodox orthography the intentional mispelling of certain dialect humorists. This corrective seems to me necessary if they are to be rescued from the oblivion to which their eccentric spelling is rapidly consigning them. We alter the spelling of Shakespeare and bring him closer to us and make him more readable. Surely we need not hesitate to do so with these lesser lights. The letter of wit, like the letter of the law, is often in sharp conflict with its spirit. So it was with these men. They were unaware that phonetic wit is auditory and not visual, and simply followed the tradition of their time. Yet how amusingly they defended it from attack. Artemus Ward declared: 'It is a pity that Chawcer, who had geneyus, was so unedicated; he's the wuss speller I know of'.

Unintentional humour has generally been omitted from this

book because the element of awareness is the *sine qua non* of wit. Nevertheless, here and there an exception has enabled a humourless creature to creep into these pages. Whitman has already been mentioned, and there is also Shelley. 'I am convinced', he wrote, 'that there can be no regeneration of mankind until laughter is put down'. Even with humorous creatures I have made an occasional exception of unintentional humour, but only when I thought such items quotable for reverse laughs. For example, Dr Johnson's polysyllabic definition of network.

This book is restricted to quotations from notable authors. Thus, comic sayings which derive from obscure authors have been omitted; also all items of anonymous origin, whether proverbs or not. This has necessitated the exclusion of famous proverbialists, such as Heywood. An exception has been made of Franklin, whose merry personality animated many a proverbial saying.

The contents have also been restricted to quotations of single-sentence length, generally to twenty-five words. To this rule, as to others, I have admitted exceptions. But I have constantly borne in mind that these quotations must be comic laconics, that their brevity is as essential as their wit, and their wit as essential as their famous authors. In detaching a quotation from its context so that it could stand alone—brief, complete, and epigrammatic—I have sometimes had to alter punctuation, omit qualifying phrases, delete proper, because unknown, names, and so on. But all such liberties I have taken have been minor ones, and in no case do they violate the original spirit or meaning.

Many immortals who flourish in quotation dictionaries and treasuries of humour are missing from this book. Poets like Milton, Keats, and Wordsworth, and others have been omitted because they had no humour in them. Famous prose writers, too, will not be found here—humourless ones like Pater and Bunyan, for example. Still others are absent, as already explained, owing to the barriers of time and translation, and the difficulty of covering contemporaries. As for the great humorists, many of them are only slightly represented here. Rabelais is among these, as well as Lewis Carroll, Cervantes,

Dickens, and even Shakespeare. The nature of this work prevents it from doing justice to authors whose humour does not reside chiefly in witty sentences.

Conversely, I am aware of having included much wittily-worded trivia. Salt and substance, like quantity and quality, do not always make laughing companions here. If certain light-weights, like Helen Rowland and Austin O'Malley, appear as heavyweights in these pages, it is due solely to their uncommon quotability. The eminently quotable are not always the quotably eminent.

This may partly explain why Oscar Wilde stands here quantitatively so far ahead of Bernard Shaw and Mark Twain. 'In all pointed sentences', declared the Great Cham of Literature, 'some degree of accuracy must be sacrificed to conciseness'. To Wilde the right angle was not some degree but more often ninety degrees, which makes so many of his witty-pretty comments more false then true. Yet they are no less amusing for that. When Shaw said, 'When a thing is funny, search it for a hidden truth', he was referring to Shavian shafts rather than the wit of Wilde. One need not go beyond this compilation for proof that much truth is said in jest—and much untruth as well. 'My way of joking', said Shaw again, 'is telling the truth; that is the funniest joke in the world'. But it is not the way of all flashes of wit. Will Rogers, too, knew that 'a gag to be good has to be fashioned about some truth. The rest you get by your slant on it, and perhaps by a wee bit of exaggeration, so's people won't miss the point'.

The special nature of these contents throws light on many matters in the field of humour. A few of these high lights are worth pointing out, but without any extended comment.

Scattered among the comic quotations are the opinions famous people have flung at others equally famous. These are often biting biographies-in-one-sentence, and they are as revealing as amusing. Under Oscar Wilde alone are listed verbal caricatures of Browning, Frank Harris, Henry James, Meredith, George Moore, Shaw, Wagner, and Whistler. If you are interested in biography, you will find the subject index profitable.

This collection also covers the facetious fancies of both

sexes. It includes more examples of the wit of women than any other reference book. By this proof, it clarifies a subject of unfailing interest—the place in humour of the daughters of Eve. The funny females who parade through these pages range alphabetically from Sophie Arnould and Jane Austen to Carolyn Wells and Rebecca West. And they represent many types of notabilities: humorists, journalists, letter writers, novelists.

Another subject of endless interest among Englishmen and Americans is the difference between their humour. A comparison of their leading wits, as exemplified here, underlines this difference. The most outstanding figure in this collection is Oscar Wilde, who is generally considered the world's greatest wit. He leads the Englishmen, followed by two great men of culture and letters, Bernard Shaw and Samuel Butler. Mark Twain is the high-water mark of American humour, and he has no close runner-up. Naturally this quantitative comparison is more suggestive than exact. Wilde and Shaw, for example, are of Irish origin. Moreover, this collection cannot throw light on those wider differences between English and American humour which exceed the single-sentence limit of epigrams.

One final word. Although this dictionary of comic quotations will be enjoyed by the random reader, it is intended even more for the reference user. Its arrangement and index make it a convenient tool for amateur wit-lovers and professional humorists. As for others, I am reminded of Bovée: 'Next to being witty yourself, the best thing to do is to be able to quote another's wit'.

EVAN ESAR

Preface to the English Edition

In re-editing this Treasury for English readers I have confined myself strictly to adjusting the balance between American and English quotations, of which the former naturally predominated in the original edition. This has involved the deletion of nearly five hundred quotations of American origin and their replacement by alternatives gathered mostly from English sources, though a few are from the works of foreign authors.

Accepting the terms prescribed by Mr Esar, I have confined my extracts as far as possible to sayings by authors or wits of established reputation, and generally speaking have kept to the limit of twenty-five words which he has laid down.

Acceptance of these terms, however, does not necessarily mean that I accept also his definitions of wit, nor, without reservation, his assessment of certain authors. Wit is as personal and as variable a thing as the liking some men have for oysters, or the dislike oysters have for some men. I would not have included, for instance, so many simple philosophers, if only because their wit is of a kind less familiar to English than to American readers. But it is not for me to shift the balance Mr Esar has struck between one American author and another. My object, as I say, has been to adjust the combined weight of American quotations against those of English and foreign authors.

Again, I would not always agree with Mr Esar on the necessity for altering punctuation, omitting qualifying phrases, and so on, and in making my own selection I have as far as possible avoided doing this. Nevertheless, within the terms of reference implied by 're-editing' I have, I hope, kept to the spirit, if not strictly to the letter, of Mr Esar's purpose.

Nicolas Bentley

The Treasury of Humorous Quotations

ADAMS, Franklin Pierce ('F.P.A.'), 1881–1960
American journalist, poet, and humorous writer.

1. Accustomed as I am to public speaking, I know the futility of it.
2. The best part of the fiction in many novels is the notice that the characters are all purely imaginary.
3. The best you get is an even break.
4. Count that day won when, turning on its axis, this earth imposes no additional taxes.
5. Don't tell me what you dream'd last night for I've been reading Freud.
6. Dunking is bad taste but tastes good.
7. A first edition of his work is a rarity but a second is rarer still.
8. Health is the thing that makes you feel that now is the best time of the year.
9. If a man keep his trap shut, the world will beat a path to his door.
10. In the order named, these are the hardest to control: Wine, Women, and Song.
11. Insomniacs don't sleep because they worry about it, and they worry about it because they don't sleep.
12. Middle age occurs when you are too young to take up golf and too old to rush up to the net.
13. She was suffering from fallen archness.
14. There are seventy stanzas in the Uruguay national anthem, which fact may account for the Uruguay standing army.
15. There's no accounting for tastes, as the woman said when somebody told her her son was wanted by the police.

16. What this country needs is a good five-cent nickel.
17. You never know what you can do without until you try.

ADAMS, Thomas, 1612–1653, *English divine and theologian.*
Those bottled windy drinks that laugh in a man's face and then cut his throat.

ADDISON, Joseph, 1672–1719
English essayist, statesman, and poet.

1. Authors have established it as a kind of rule that a man ought to be dull sometimes.
2. A moneylender serves you in the present tense, lends you in the conditional mood, keeps you in the subjunctive, and ruins you in the future.
3. Nothing is capable of being well set to music that is not nonsense.
4. There is not so variable a thing in Nature as a lady's head-dress.
5. We are always doing something for posterity, but I would fain see posterity do something for us.
6. A woman seldom asks advice before she has bought her wedding clothes.

ADE, George, 1866–1944
American humorous author and playwright.

1. After being turned down by numerous publishers, he decided to write for posterity.
2. Anybody can win, unless there happens to be a second entry.
3. Don't try to marry an entire family or it may work out that way.
4. Early to bed and early to rise, and you'll meet very few of our best people.
5. For parlor use, the vague generality is a lifesaver.
6. A friend who is very near and dear may in time become as useless as a relative.
7. A good folly is worth whatever you pay for it.
8. A good musical comedy consists largely of disorderly conduct occasionally interrupted by talk.

9. He had been kicked in the head by a mule when young, and believed everything he read in the Sunday papers.
10. He had heard that one is permitted a certain latitude with widows, and went in for the whole 180 degrees.
11. Here's to man: he can afford anything he can get; here's to woman: she can afford anything she can get a man to get for her.
12. Her features did not seem to know the value of teamwork.
13. The house was more covered with mortgages than with paint.
14. If it were not for the presents, an elopement would be preferable.
15. The music teacher came twice each week to bridge the awful gap between Dorothy and Chopin.
16. My father sent me to an engineering school to prepare me for a literary career.
17. She invariably was first over the fence in the mad pursuit of culture.
18. She told him it was terrible to hear such things as he told her and to please go ahead.
19. She was a town-and-country soprano of the kind often used for augmenting the grief at a funeral.
20. She was short on intellect, but long on shape.
21. There are only three basic jokes, but since the mother-in-law joke is not a joke but a very serious question, there are only two.
22. Those who marry to escape something usually find something else.
23. The time to enjoy a European trip is about three weeks after unpacking.
24. 'Whom are you?' said he, for he had been to night school.

ADLER, Alfred, 1870–1937

Austrian psychologist and psychiatrist.

It is easier to fight one's principles than to live up to them.

AGASSIZ, Louis J. R., 1807–1873

Swiss-American zoologist and geologist.

I cannot afford to waste my time making money.

AGATE, James, 1877–1947, *English dramatic critic.*

1. The capacity for genius and the capacity for getting that genius recognised are two quite different things.
2. The English instinctively admire any man who has no talent and is modest about it.
3. The great works can never do any harm to a mind which, having no impression at all, can have no false impressions.
4. I have views on most matters, and am as willing as a politician to change most of them.
5. It has always been said that money talks, but I rather think that it is beginning to talk too loudly.
6. Long experience has taught me that in England nobody goes to the theatre unless he or she has bronchitis.
7. Respectability is in itself no bar to the production of works of art.
8. Though great artists have been licentious, licence does not necessarily result in great art.
9. To force myself to earn more money, I determined to spend more.

AINSLIE, Douglas, 1865–1948
English poet, critic, and philosopher.

You can never trust a woman; she may be true to you.

ALDINGTON, Richard, 1892–1962
English poet, novelist, and critic.

Nationalism is a silly cock crowing on its own dunghill.

ALEXANDER the Great, 356–323 B.C.
King of Macedonia, conqueror of Greece, Egypt, and Persia.

I am dying with the help of too many physicians.

ALLEN, Fred, 1894–1956, *American radio comedian.*

1. Advertising agency: eighty-five per cent confusion and fifteen per cent commission.
2. An associate producer is the only guy in Hollywood who will associate with a producer.

3. California is a fine place to live in—if you happen to be an orange.
4. A conference is a gathering of important people who singly can do nothing, but together can decide that nothing can be done.
5. He dreamed he was eating Shredded Wheat and woke up to find the mattress half gone.
6. He is so narrow-minded that if he fell on a pin, it would blind him in both eyes.
7. He pasted picture postcards around goldfish bowls to make the goldfish think they were going places.
8. He was not brought by the stork; he was delivered by a man from the Audubon Society personally.
9. Her hat is a creation that will never go out of style; it will just look ridiculous year after year.
10. His hobby is collecting old echoes.
11. Hollywood is a place where people from Iowa mistake each other for movie stars.
12. Hollywood is no place for a professional comedian; the amateur competition is too great.
13. I have never seen a pair of slacks that had very much slack in them.
14. I like long walks, especially when they are taken by people who annoy me.
15. I play a musical instrument some, but only for my own amazement.
16. If a circus is half as good as it smells, it's a great show.
17. Man has made his bedlam; let him lie in it.
18. The man was so small, he was a waste of skin.
19. My agent gets ten per cent of everything I get, except my blinding headaches.
20. On ships they call them barnacles; in radio they attach themselves to desks, and are called vice-presidents.
21. The only thing he ever takes out on a moonlit night is his upper plate.
22. Sense doesn't make sense in radio.
23. Some movie stars wear their sunglasses even in church; they're afraid God might recognize them and ask for autographs.

24. What's on your mind—if you'll forgive the overstatement
25. When you smoke cigarettes you're likely to burn yourself to death; with chewing tobacco the worst thing you can do is drown a midget.

ALLEN, Grant, 1848–1899, *British author of voluminous fiction.*

1. All men are born free and unequal.
2. Cockroaches think that kitchens were created to afford a convenient home for cockroaches.

ANACHARSIS, c. 600 B.C., *Scythian philosopher.*

The market is a place set apart where men may deceive each other.

ARBUTHNOT, John, 1667–1735

Scottish physician and political pamphleteer.

1. All political parties die at last of swallowing their own lies.
2. Biography is one of the new terrors of death.

ARETINO, Pietro, 1492–1556, *Italian satirist.*

1. If you want to annoy your neighbours, tell the truth about them.
2. Wise is the young man who is always thinking of taking a wife, and never takes one.

ARISTOTLE, 384–322 B.C.

Greek philosopher, student of Plato, and teacher of Alexander the Great.

1. Homer has taught all other poets the art of telling lies skilfully.
2. My friends! There are no friends.

ARLEN, Michael, 1895–1956, *British novelist and playwright.*

1. It is amazing how nice people are to you when they know you are going away.
2. She not only expects the worst, but makes the worst of it when it happens.

ARNOLD, Matthew, 1822–1888, *English poet and critic.*

1. One has often wondered whether . . . there is anything so unintelligent, so unapt to perceive how the world is really going, as an ordinary young Englishman of our upper class.
2. We have got three distinct terms, Barbarians, Philistines, Populace, to denote roughly the great classes into which our society is divided.

ARNOULD, Sophie, 1744–1802, *French opera star and wit.*

1. Oh! the good old days when I was so unhappy.
2. Women give themselves to God when the devil wants nothing more to do with them.

AUDEN, Wystan Hugh, born 1907, *English poet.*

A professor is one who talks in someone else's sleep.

AUERBACH, Berthold, 1812–1882, *German novelist.*

What's all our knowledge worth? We don't even know what the weather will be tomorrow.

AUGUSTINE, Saint, A.D. 354–430

One of the leaders in the early Christian Church.

1. Give me chastity and self-restraint, but do not give it yet.
2. The playthings of our elders are called business.
3. To abstain from sin when a man cannot sin is to be forsaken by sin, not to forsake it.

AUSTEN, Jane, 1775–1817, *English novelist.*

1. I have been a selfish being all my life, in practice, though not in principle.
2. A woman, especially, if she have the misfortune of knowing anything, should conceal it as well as she can.

BACON, Francis, Lord Verulam, 1561–1626

English statesman, philosopher, and essayist.

1. The French are wiser than they seem, and the Spaniards seem wiser than they are.
2. Silence is the virtue of fools, so . . . if you are wise, you are a fool; if you are a fool, you are wise.

BAER, Arthur ('Bugs'), 1897?–1969

American comic columnist and short-story writer.

1. Alimony is like buying oats for a dead horse.
2. Although it is a far cry from there to here, he laughed all the way.
3. An empty cab drove up, and Sarah Bernhardt got out.
4. Do incubator chickens love their mother?
5. A good neighbour is a fellow who smiles at you over the back fence but doesn't climb over it.
6. He doesn't remember any silent days in motion pictures—the director always yelled.
7. He had insomnia so bad that he couldn't sleep when he was working.
8. He had reasons for not working; he said your body was only a machine and he was no mechanic.
9. He is an adventurer who traces leaky plumbing to its source.
10. He was so ugly, the last time I saw him he was the top of a totem pole in Seattle.
11. He was born silly and had a relapse.
12. He was thrown out trying to steal second; his head was full of larceny but his feet were honest.
13. He writes dialogues by cutting monologues in two.
14. Hello! We heard you at the door, but just thought you were part of the bad weather.
15. His family were the largest dandruff manufacturers in France.
16. How much would you charge to haunt a house?
17. I paused like a woodpecker at timber line.
18. If you do big things they print your face, and if you do little things they only print your thumbs.
19. If you laid all our laws end to end, there would be no end.
20. It arrived by first-class mail in second-class condition.

It is impossible to tell where the law stops and justice begins.

22. It was as helpful as throwing a drowning man both ends of a rope.
23. It was so quiet, you could hear a pun drop.

24. The ladies looked one another over with microscopic carelessness.
25. A newspaper is a circulating library with high blood pressure.
26. She's always in a triangle—like Napoleon's hat.
27. She's generous to a fault—if it's her own.
28. She used to diet on any kind of food she could lay her hands on.
29. She was a brunette by birth but a blonde by habit.
30. She was always crying; in fact, she wept so much she made everybody's corns ache.
31. What did the storm at sea say to the passenger's lunch?
32. You can always judge a man by what he eats, and therefore a country in which there is no free lunch is no longer a free country.
33. You can take a boy out of the country but you can't take the country out of a boy.

BAGEHOT, Walter, 1826–1877

English economist, essayist, and journalist.

1. The cure for admiring the House of Lords is to go and look at it.
2. The great pleasure in life is doing what people say you cannot do.
3. The greatest mistake is trying to be more agreeable than you can be.
4. The House of Peers has never been a House where the most important peers were most important.
5. Human nature is not a high thing, but at least it has a high idea of itself.
6. An inability to stay quiet is one of the most conspicuous failings of mankind.
7. It is good to be without vice, but it is not good to be without temptations.
8. Men who do not make advances to women are apt to become victims to women who make advances to them.
9. The most melancholy of human reflections, perhaps, is that, on the whole, it is a question whether the benevolence of man does most harm or good.

10. One of the greatest pains to human nature is the pain of a new idea.
11. A parliament is nothing less than a big meeting of more or less idle people.
12. Poverty is an anomaly to rich people; it is very difficult to make out why people who want dinner do not ring the bell.
13. Throughout the greater part of his life George III was a kind of 'consecrated obstruction'.

BAILEY, Philip James, 1816–1902, *English poet and lawyer.*

The worst men often give the best advice.

BALFOUR, Arthur James, Earl of, 1848–1930
English statesman and philosopher.

1. Frank Harris . . . said . . . 'The fact is, Mr. Balfour, all the faults of our age come from Christianity and journalism'. Christianity, of course, but why journalism?
2. I thought he was a young man of promise, but it appears he is a young man of promises.
3. It is unfortunate, considering that enthusiasm moves the world, that so few enthusiasts can be trusted to speak the truth.

BALZAC, Honoré de, 1799–1850, *French novelist.*

1. Believe everything you hear about the world; nothing is too impossibly bad.
2. Friendships last when each friend thinks he has a slight superiority over the other.
3. A good husband is never the first to go to sleep at night or the last to awake in the morning.
4. A husband should always know what is the matter with his wife, for she always knows what is not.
5. I do not regard a broker as a member of the human race.
6. If we all said to people's faces what we say behind each other's backs, society would be impossible.
7. Marriage is the end of man.
8. Money brings everything to you, even your daughters.

9. Nature makes only dull animals; we owe the fool to society.
10. One of the first conditions of learning in a woman is to keep the fact a profound secret.
11. When a woman gets too old to be attractive to man she turns to God.
12. When in Turkey, do as the turkeys do.
13. When there is an old maid in the house, a watchdog is unnecessary.
14. Women, when they have made a sheep of a man, always tell him that he is a lion with a will of iron.

BANGS, John Kendrick, 1862–1922
American humorous writer and lecturer.

1. All press agents belong to a club of which Ananias is the honorary president.
2. Although man is already ninety per cent water, the Prohibitionists are not yet satisfied.
3. Being an Episcopalian interferes neither with my business nor my religion.
4. I can't tell a lie—not even when I hear one.
5. Pandemonium did not reign; it poured.
6. She would rather fool with a bee than be with a fool.

BARHAM, Richard Harris, 1788–1845
English divine and author of The Ingoldsby Legends.

There, too, many an aldermanic nose, roll'd its loud diapason after dinner.

BARNUM, Phineas Taylor, 1810–1891, *American showman.*

1. Every crowd has a silver lining.
2. There's a sucker born every minute.

BARRIE, James Matthew, 1860–1937
Scottish dramatist and novelist.

1. Every man who is high up loves to think that he has done it all himself; and the wife smiles, and lets it go at that.
2. God gave us our memories so that we might have roses in December.

3. The God to whom little boys say their prayers has a face very like their mother's.
4. Have you ever noticed that many jewels make women either incredibly fat or incredibly thin?
5. His lordship may compel us to be equal upstairs, but there will never be equality in the servants' hall.
6. I'm a second eleven sort of chap.
7. I am not young enough to know everything.
8. If *Hamlet* had been written in these days it would probably have been called *The Strange Affair at Elsinore*.
9. It's grand, and you canna' expect to be baith grand and comfortable.
10. It is not true that woman was made from man's rib; she was really made from his funny bone.
11. Never ascribe to an opponent motives meaner than your own.
12. There are few more impressive sights in the world than a Scotsman on the make.
13. The printing press is either the greatest blessing or the greatest curse of modern times, one sometimes forgets which.
14. She was a large woman who seemed not so much dressed as upholstered.
15. We are all of us failures—at least, the best of us are.

BARRY, Gerald, 1898–1968, *English editor and publicist.*

Democracy: in which you say what you like and do what you're told.

BARRYMORE, John, 1882–1942, *American actor.*

1. America is the country where you buy a lifetime supply of aspirin for one dollar, and use it up in two weeks.
2. The good die young—because they see it's no use living if you've got to be good.
3. I am thinking about taking a fifth wife; why not? Solomon had a thousand wives and he is a synonym for wisdom.
4. I've read some of your modern free verse and wonder who set it free.
5. If it isn't the sheriff, it's the finance company; I've got more attachments on me than a vacuum cleaner.

6. In Genesis it says that it is not good for a man to be alone but sometimes it is a great relief.
7. Love is the delightful interval between meeting a beautiful girl and discovering that she looks like a haddock.
8. My wife is the kind of girl who'll not go anywhere without her mother, and her mother will go anywhere.
9. My wife was too beautiful for words, but not for arguments.
10. One of my chief regrets during my years in the theater is that I couldn't sit in the audience and watch me.
11. Paper napkins never return from a laundry, nor love from a trip to the law courts.
12. There's something about a closet that makes a skeleton terribly restless.
13. The thing that takes up the least amount of time and causes the most amount of trouble is Sex.
14. The trouble with life is that there are so many beautiful women and so little time.
15. The way to fight a woman is with your hat—grab it and run.
16. You never realize how short a month is until you pay alimony.

BARSLEY, Michael, born 1913
English humorist and radio writer.

Debentures and Debutantes can both make a man happy, if they give him sufficient control.

BARUCH, Bernard Mannes, 1870–1965
American statesman and financier.

To me, old age is always fifteen years older than I am.

BASON, Fred, born 1907, *English bookseller and author.*

His wife is so mean that if he gave her a crutch, she'd go and break her bloody leg.

BAUDELAIRE, Pierre Charles, 1821–1867
French poet and critic.

1. Life is a hospital in which every patient is possessed by the desire to change his bed.

2. The man who gets on best with women is the one who knows best how to get on without them.
3. A sweetheart is a bottle of wine; a wife is a wine bottle.
4. What is love? The need to escape from oneself.

BEAUMARCHAIS, Caron de, 1732–1799, *French playwright.*

1. It is not necessary to understand things in order to argue about them.
2. You have given yourself the trouble to be born.

BECKFORD, William, 1759–1844
English writer and art collector.

He did not think . . . that it was necessary to make a hell of this world to enjoy paradise in the next.

BEECHER, Henry Ward, 1813–1887
American preacher, lecturer, and reformer.

1. The cynic puts all human actions into two classes: openly bad and secretly bad.
2. Every man should have a fair-sized cemetery in which to bury the faults of his friends.
3. Flowers are the sweetest things that God ever made and forgot to put a soul into.
4. Men are called fools in one age for not knowing what they were called fools for averring in the age before.
5. The monkey is an organized sarcasm upon the human race.
6. Next to ingratitude, the most painful thing to bear is gratitude.
7. Poverty is very good in poems but very bad in the house; very good in maxims and sermons but very bad in practical life.
8. Selfishness is that detestable vice which no one will forgive in others and no one is without in himself.
9. Some people are so dry that you might soak them in a joke for a month and it would not get through their skins.
10. There are many people who think that Sunday is a sponge to wipe out all the sins of the week.

BEERBOHM, Sir Max, 1872–1956
English essayist and caricaturist.

1. 'After all', as a pretty girl once said to me, 'women are a sex by themselves, so to speak'.
2. Fate wrote her a most tremendous tragedy, and she played it in tights.
3. I was a modest, good-humoured boy. It is Oxford that has made me insufferable.
4. People are either born hosts or born guests.
5. Suspicion slid down the bannisters of his mind, trailing a blue ribbon. Inebriates were one of his hobbies.
6. To give an accurate and exhaustive account of that period would need a far less brilliant pen than mine.

BEHN, Aphra, 1640–1689, *English dramatist and novelist.*

1. Come away; poverty's catching.
2. He that will live in this world must be endowed with the three rare qualities of dissimulation, equivocation, and mental reservation.
3. Money speaks sense in a language all nations understand.

BELLOC, Hilaire, 1870–1953
English novelist, poet, and essayist.

1. Birds in their little nests agree with Chinamen, but not with me.
2. The Socratic manner is not a game at which two can play.
3. With an indolent expression and an undulating throat, like an unsuccessful literary man.

BENCHLEY, Robert, 1889–1945
American humorous editor, critic, actor, and author.

1. Drawing on my fine command of language, I said nothing.
2. Drinking makes such fools of people, and people are such fools to begin with, that it's compounding a felony.
3. I do most of my work sitting down; that's where I shine.
4. In America there are two classes of travel—first class, and with children.
5. It took me fifteen years to discover I had no talent for writing, but I couldn't give it up because by that time I was too famous.

6. It was one of those plays in which all the actors unfortunately enunciated very clearly.

BENNETT, Arnold, 1867–1931, *English novelist and playwright.*

1. Being a husband is a whole-time job. That is why so many husbands fail. They cannot give their entire attention to it.
2. A cause may be inconvenient, but it's magnificent. It's like champagne or high shoes, and one must be prepared to suffer for it.
3. Good taste is better than bad taste, but bad taste is better than no taste at all.
4. His opinion of himself, having once risen, remained at 'set fair'.
5. It is a profound truth that women as a sex are vain; it is also a profound truth that men as a sex are vain.
6. It is only people of small moral stature who have to stand on their dignity.
7. It is well, when one is judging a friend, to remember that he is judging you with the same godlike and superior impartiality.
8. Journalists say a thing that they know isn't true, in the hope that if they keep on saying it long enough it *will* be true.
9. Make love to every woman you meet; if you get five per cent on your outlay, it's a good investment.
10. A man of sixty has spent twenty years in bed and over three years in eating.
11. Pessimism, when you get used to it, is just as agreeable as optimism.
12. Women are strange and incomprehensible, a device invented by Providence to keep the wit of man well sharpened by constant employment.

BENNETT, James Gordon, 1841–1918
American newspaper editor.

I have made mistakes, but I have never made the mistake of claiming that I never made one.

BENTHAM, Jeremy, 1748–1832

English philosopher, jurist, and political scientist.

Lawyers are the only persons in whom ignorance of the law is not punished.

BENTLEY, Edmund Clerihew, 1875–1956

English journalist and author.

1. He had . . . an ironical suavity that was much appreciated by those who were not the subjects of it
2. Ill-health is one of the things that appeal most irresistibly to the popular sense of humour.

BENTLEY, Nicolas, born 1907

English humorous artist and author.

1. The argument became so heated that the woman next door sent for the fire brigade.
2. The French will tell you there is no such thing as English chic. They are wrong. I know several women who suffer from it.
3. Getting married is a serious matter for a girl; not getting married is even more serious.
4. Half a life is better than no breath.
5. He followed in his father's footsteps, but his gait was somewhat erratic.
6. He who enjoys a good neighbour, said the Greeks, has a precious possession. Same goes for the neighbour's wife.
7. Her interest in natural history was confined to observation of the crow's feet gathering round her eyes.
8. His was the sort of career that made the Recording Angel think seriously about taking up shorthand.
9. It is the unshakeable sincerity of the Englishman's belief in his own superiority which is at once the strength and weakness of his race.
10. Many reasons have been put forward to account for Napoleon's fame, apart from those put forward by Napoleon himself.
11. Mediocrity, as Alma-Tadema discovered, has its compensations.
12. No news is good news; no journalists is even better.

13. One should not exaggerate the importance of trifles. Life, for instance, is much too short to be taken seriously.
14. An onion will make me cry, but the only vegetable I have ever found to make me laugh is my sister-in-law.

BERANGER, Pierre Jean de, 1780–1857
French poet and song writer.

In spite of their hats being terribly ugly, God Damn! I love the English!

BETHELL, Richard, Baron Westbury, 1800–1873
English Lord Chancellor.

You will turn it over once more in what you are pleased to call your mind.

BICKERSTAFFE, Isaac, 1735?–1812?, *Irish dramatist.*

Perhaps it was right to dissemble your love. But—why did you kick me downstairs?

BIERCE, Ambrose, 1842–1914?
American short-story writer and journalist.

1. Abstainer: a weak person who yields to the temptation of denying himself a pleasure.
2. Acquaintance: a degree of friendship called slight when its object is poor or obscure, and intimate when he is rich or famous.
3. Acquaintance: a person whom we know well enough to borrow from, but not well enough to lend to.
4. Admiration: our polite recognition of another man's resemblance to ourselves.
5. All are lunatics, but he who can analyze his delusion is called a philosopher.
6. Applause is the echo of a platitude.
7. Architect: one who drafts a plan of your house, and plans a draft of your money.
8. Armor is the kind of clothing worn by a man whose tailor was a blacksmith.
9. Bore: a person who talks when you wish him to listen.
10. Brain: the apparatus with which we think we think.
11. Cabbage: a familiar kitchen-garden vegetable about as large and wise as a man's head.

12. Calamities are of two kinds: misfortune to ourselves, and good fortune to others.
13. Christians and camels receive their burdens kneeling.
14. A clergyman is a man who undertakes the management of our spiritual affairs as a method of bettering his temporal ones.
15. A conservative is a statesman who is enamored of existing evils, as distinguished from the liberal who wishes to replace them with others.
16. Coward: one who in a perilous emergency thinks with his legs.
17. Cynic: a blackguard whose faulty vision sees things as they are, not as they ought to be.
18. Dentist: a prestidigitator who, putting metal into your mouth, pulls coins out of your pocket.
19. Diaphragm: a muscular partition separating disorders of the chest from disorders of the bowels.
20. Discussion: a method of confirming others in their errors.
21. Don't steal. Thou'lt never thus compete successfully in business. Cheat.
22. Education: that which discloses to the wise and disguises from the foolish their lack of understanding.
23. Egotist: a person of low taste, more interested in himself than in me.
24. Empty wine bottles have a bad opinion of women.
25. Experience is a revelation in the light of which we renounce our errors of youth for those of age.
26. The fact that boys are allowed to exist at all is evidence of a remarkable Christian forbearance among men.
27. Faith: belief without evidence in what is told by one who speaks without knowledge, of things without parallel.
28. Fashion: a despot whom the wise ridicule and obey.
29. The first man you meet is a fool; if you do not think so ask him, and he will prove it.
30. The gambling known as business looks with austere disfavor upon the business known as gambling.
31. Genealogy: an account of one's descent from an ancestor who did not particularly care to trace his own.

2

32. The hardest tumble a man can make is to fall over his own bluff.
33. Here's to woman! Would that we could fall into her arms without falling into her hands.
34. History: an account mostly false, of events unimportant, which are brought about by rulers mostly knaves, and soldiers mostly fools.
35. Hospitality: the virtue which induces us to feed and lodge certain persons who are not in need of food and lodging.
36. In each human heart are a tiger, a pig, an ass, and a nightingale; diversity of character is due to their unequal activity.
37. Lecturer: one with his hand in your pocket, his tongue in your ear, and his faith in your patience.
38. Marriage: the state or condition of a community consisting of a master, a mistress, and two slaves, making, in all, two.
39. Of two evils, choose to be the least.
40. Opportunity: a favorable occasion for grasping a disappointment.
41. Our vocabulary is defective; we give the same name to woman's lack of temptation and man's lack of opportunity.
42. Peace: in international affairs, a period of cheating between two periods of fighting.
43. Positive: being mistaken at the top of one's voice.
44. A prejudice is a vagrant opinion without visible means of support.
45. Revolution: in politics, an abrupt change in the form of misgovernment.
46. A saint is a dead sinner revised and edited.
47. Slang is the speech of him who robs the literary garbage cans on their way to the dump.
48. Take not God's name in vain; select a time when it will have effect.
49. To apologize is to lay the foundation for a future offense.
50. To the small part of ignorance that we arrange and classify we give the name knowledge.

51. Total abstainer: one who abstains from everything but abstention, and especially from inactivity in the affairs of others.
52. When Eve saw her reflection in a pool, she sought Adam and accused him of infidelity.
53. When you are ill make haste to forgive your enemies, for you may recover.
54. You are not permitted to kill a woman who has injured you, but nothing forbids you to reflect that she is growing older every minute.

BILLINGS, Josh, 1818–1885

Pseudonym of Henry Wheeler Shaw, American humorist.

1. The best medicine I know for rheumatism is to thank the Lord it ain't the gout.
2. The best way to convince a fool that he is wrong is to let him have his own way.
3. Confess your sins to the Lord, and you will be forgiven; confess them to men, and you will be laughed at.
4. Don't despise your poor relations; they may become suddenly rich someday.
5. Experience increases our wisdom but doesn't reduce our follies.
6. Give the devil his due, but be very careful that there ain't much due him.
7. I have finally come to the conclusion that a good reliable set of bowels is worth more to a man than any quantity of brains.
8. If the animals had reason, they would act just as ridiculous as we menfolks do.
9. If you want to get a sure crop, and a big yield, sow wild oats.
10. When a man comes to me for advice, I find out the kind of advice he wants, and I give it to him.

BINSTEAD, Arthur M., 1861–1914

English humorous author and sporting journalist.

1. All barmaids who are not fools are philosophers.

2. Every singer in a village quartette can give you three good reasons why the organisation isn't absolutely perfect.
3. A fine, handsome specimen of British manhood, standing every bit of six foot two in his shoes, and fearing nothing but closing time.
4. He was pleasanter than original sin.
5. She should have been more careful to master the art of walking on eggs without breaking them.
6. There is a tide in the affairs of young men, which, if not skilfully dodged, effectually drowns them.
7. . . . two gentlemen whose cast of features involuntarily reminded one of the only recorded instance of the Red Sea being crossed on foot.
8. A young man with burnt umber hands and saffron finger nails, fading away, possibly, to deeper chemical shades up towards his shoulder blades.

BIRRELL, Augustine, 1850–1933, *English essayist and critic.*

1. Englishmen have ever loved precedents, even in their love letters.
2. Of all odd crazes, the craze to be forever reading new books is one of the oddest.

BISMARCK, Otto von, 1815–1898, *German statesman.*

1. Be polite; write diplomatically; even in a declaration of war one observes the rules of politeness.
2. I have seen three emperors in their nakedness, and the sight was not inspiring.

BLACKIE, John Stuart, 1809–1895
Scottish author and translator.

Wine is the drink of the gods, milk the drink of babies, tea the drink of women, and water the drink of beasts.

BLAKE, William, 1757–1827, *English poet and painter.*

Do be my enemy—for friendship's sake.

BLESSINGTON, Marguerite, Countess of, 1789–1849
English novelist.

1. Friends are the Thermometers by which one may judge the temperature of our fortunes.
2. Love-matches are made by people who are content, for a month of honey, to condemn themselves to a life of vinegar.

BOHN, Henry George, 1796–1884
English publisher and bookseller.

1. A good occasion of courtship is when the widow returns from the funeral.
2. May the man be damned and never grow fat who wears two faces under one hat.

BOLITHO, William, 1890–1930, *English author.*

The shortest way out of Manchester is notoriously a bottle of Gordon's gin.

BOSSUET, Jacques, 1627–1704
French theologian and preacher.

The cruellest revenge of a woman is to remain faithful to a man.

BOUCICAULT, Dion, 1822–1890
Irish-Anglo-American dramatist and actor.

I wish Adam had died with all his ribs in his body.

BOURGET, Paul, 1852–1935, *French poet, novelist, and critic.*

The proof that experience teaches us nothing is that the end of one love does not prevent us from beginning another.

BRADLEY, Francis Herbert, 1846–1924
English writer on philosophy.

1. Everything comes to him who waits—among other things, death.
2. His mind is open; yes, it is so open that nothing is retained; ideas simply pass through him.

3. Metaphysics is the finding of bad reasons for what we believe on instinct.
4. Optimism: the world is the best of all possible worlds, and everything in it is a necessary evil.
5. Pessimism: where everything is bad, it must be good to know the worst.
6. The propriety of some persons seems to consist in having improper thoughts about their neighbours.
7. There are those who so dislike the nude that they find something indecent in the naked truth.

BRETON, Nicholas, 1545?–1626?, *English poet.*

Money makes the old mare trot and the young tit amble.

BRILLAT-SAVARIN, Anthelme, 1755–1826
French politician and writer on gastronomy.

The table is the only place where a man is never bored during the first hour.

BROOKE, Rupert, 1887–1915, *English poet.*

1. . . . Cambridge people rarely smile. Being urban, squat and packed with guile.
2. On lissom, clerical, printless toe.
3. The sly shade of a Rural Dean.

BROUGHAM, Henry, 1778–1868
British statesman, author, and scholar.

A lawyer is a learned gentleman who rescues your estate from your enemies and keeps it himself.

BROUN, Heywood, 1888–1939
American journalist and columnist.

1. The ability to make love frivolously is the chief characteristic which distinguishes human beings from the beasts.
2. Christian ethics are seldom found save in the philosophy of some unbeliever.
3. God is always on the side which has the best football coach.
4. If anyone corrects your pronunciation of a word in a public place, you have every right to punch him in the nose.

5. It is always safe to be dogmatic about tomorrow.
6. Repartee is what you wish you'd said.
7. The urge to gamble is so universal and its practice so pleasurable that I assume it must be evil.
8. What a dull world this would be if every imaginative maker of legends was stigmatized as a liar!

BROWN, Ivor, born 1891, *English author and critic.*

He undertook to shield the children of advanced parents from the horrors of education.

BROWN, Thomas Edward, 1830–1897, *Manx poet.*

A rich man's joke is always funny.

BROWNE, Sir Thomas, 1605–1682
English writer and physician.

1. The long habit of living indisposeth us for dying.
2. Man is a noble animal, splendid in ashes, pompous in the grave.
3. There are many (questionless) canonized on earth, that shall never be Saints in Heaven.
4. We all labour against our own cure, for death is the cure of all diseases.
5. The world, which took but six days to make, is like to take us six thousand years to make out.

BROWNING, Robert, 1812–1889, *English poet.*

1. Any nose May ravage with impunity a Rose.
2. That sallow, virgin-minded, studious Martyr to mild enthusiasm.

BRYCE, James, 1838–1922
British statesman, diplomat, historian, and writer on government.

Medicine is the only profession that labours incessantly to destroy the reason for its own existence.

BUCHAN, John, 1875–1940, *Scottish writer and historian.*

An atheist is a man who has no invisible means of support.

BUCHANAN, Robert, 1841–1901, *English poet and novelist.*

His brains were only candle-grease, and wasted down like tallow.

BUCK, Pearl, born 1892, *American novelist.*

We send missionaries to China so the Chinese can get to heaven, but we won't let them into our country.

BUNNER, Henry Cuyler, 1855–1896

American humorous writer of short stories and light verse.

Shakespeare was a dramatist of note who lived by writing things to quote.

BURBANK, Luther, 1849–1926

American naturalist, originator of new fruits and flowers.

1. For those who do not think, it is best at least to rearrange their prejudices once in a while.
2. It is well for people who think to change their minds occasionally in order to keep them clean.

BURDETTE, Robert Jones, 1844–1914

American clergyman, humorous journalist, and lecturer.

1. Don't believe the world owes you a living; the world owes you nothing—it was here first.
2. I will be so polite to my wife as though she were a perfect stranger.
3. There are two days about which nobody should ever worry, and these are yesterday and tomorrow.
4. When you are climbing a mountain, don't talk; silence gives ascent.

BURGESS, Gelett, 1866–1951

American humorous writer and illustrator.

1. Bad manners simply indicate that you care a good deal more for the food than for the society at the table.
2. If the Lord would only send something interesting, I wouldn't mind if it was only a plaid pig.

3. Many people live alone and like it, but most of them live alone and look it.
4. Men like to pursue an elusive woman, like a cake of wet soap in a bathtub—even men who hate baths.
5. She was only sixteen; but what does that matter when one is young.
6. Some men give their blood to their country; others their spleen.
7. To be two years a widow exceedeth a college education.
8. With a man, a lie is a last resort; with women, it's First Aid.

BURKE, Edmund, 1729–1797
English statesman and political writer.

1. The age of chivalry is gone; that of sophisters, economists, and calculators has succeeded.
2. He was not merely a chip off the old block, but the old block itself.
3. It is a general popular error to suppose the loudest complainers for the public to be the most anxious for its welfare.
4. Strip majesty of its exteriors (the first and last letters) and it becomes a jest.
5. They defend their errors as if they were defending their inheritance.

BURNS, Robert, 1759–1796, *Scottish poet.*

Her nose and chin they threaten ither.

BURTON, Robert, 1577–1640, *English philosopher and author.*

1. Diogenes struck the father when the son swore.
2. One was never married, and that's his hell; another is, and that's his plague.
3. They are proud in humility, proud in that they are not proud.

BUTLER, Nicholas Murray, 1862–1947, *American educator.*

1. An expert is one who knows more and more about less and less.

2. One of the embarrassments of being a gentleman is that you are not permitted to be violent in asserting your rights.

BUTLER, Samuel, 1835–1902, *English novelist and satirist.*

1. All of the animals except man know that the principal business of life is to enjoy it.
2. Any fool can paint a picture, but it takes a wise man to be able to sell it.
3. Any fool can tell the truth, but it requires a man of some sense to know how to lie well.
4. An apology for the devil: it must be remembered that we have heard only one side of the case; God has written all the books.
5. The artist drew a great many lines and saved the best of them.
6. At any rate there will be no wedding presents in heaven.
7. The better part of valour is indiscretion.
8. The body is but a pair of pincers set over a bellows and a stewpan, and the whole fixed upon stilts.
9. Books should be tried by a judge and jury as though they were crimes, and counsel should be heard on both sides.
10. Brevity is very good when we are, or are not, understood.
11. Brigands demand your money or your life; women require both.
12. Cleanliness is almost as bad as godliness.
13. Cooking is half digesting; we do half our digestion, therefore, outside our own bodies.
14. The dead being the majority, it is natural we should have more friends among them than among the living.
15. A degenerate nobleman, or one that is proud of his birth, is like a turnip; there is nothing good of him but that which is underground.
16. The devil tempted Christ, but it was Christ who tempted the devil to tempt him.
17. The dons are too busy educating the young men to be able to teach them anything.
18. For the better cure of vice they think it necessary to study it, and the only efficient study is through practice.

19. The giraffe must get up at six in the morning if it wants to have its breakfast in its stomach by nine.
20. God cannot alter the past; that is why he is obliged to connive at the existence of historians.
21. Greater luck hath no man than this, that he lay down his wife at the right moment.
22. He is considered the most graceful speaker who can say nothing in most words.
23. He was an unprincipled, principle-ridden prig.
24. He was born stupid, and greatly increased his birthright.
25. He was capable of bringing out an expurgated edition of Wordsworth.
26. A hen is only an egg's way of making another egg.
27. 'Home, Sweet Home' must surely have been written by a bachelor.
28. I do not mind lying, but I hate inaccuracy.
29. I keep my books at the British Museum and at Mudie's.
30. I should like to add an eighth sacrament to those of the Roman Church—the sacrament of Divorce.
31. I take it that all plants feel, but some make more fuss about their feelings than others.
32. If God considered woman a helpmeet for man, he must have had a very poor opinion of man.
33. If I were to say all the unpleasant things that occur to me about posthumous memoirs, I should have nothing left for my posthumous memoirs.
34. If you aim at imperfection, there is some chance of your getting it; whereas if you aim at perfection, there is none.
35. If you follow reason far enough it always leads to conclusions that are contrary to reason.
36. Invention is the mother of necessity.
37. It costs a lot of money to die comfortably.
38. It is my relations with my relations that I sometimes find embarrassing.
39. Life is one long process of getting tired.
40. Life is the art of drawing sufficient conclusions from insufficient premises.
41. A little cooking is good because it unsettles the meat's mind and prepares it for new ideas.

42. A little knowledge is a dangerous thing, but a little want of knowledge is also a dangerous thing.
43. Lord, I do not believe; help thou my unbelief.
44. Man is the only animal that can remain on friendly terms with the victims he intends to eat until he eats them.
45. A man should be just cultured enough to be able to look with suspicion upon culture.
46. Men should not try to overstrain their goodness more than any other faculty.
47. The money that men make lives after them.
48. The most important service rendered by the press is that of educating people to approach printed matter with distrust.
49. Most of those who call themselves artists are in reality picture dealers, only they make the pictures themselves.
50. Not only is there a skeleton is every closet, but there is a screw loose in every skeleton.
51. Nothing is potent against love save only impotence.
52. Nothing makes a man or woman look so saintly as seasickness.
53. The oldest books are only just out to those who have not read them.
54. The one serious conviction that a man should have is that nothing is to be taken too seriously.
55. People should learn to lie as they learn anything else—from very small beginnings.
56. Peter remained on friendly terms with Christ notwithstanding Christ's having healed his mother-in-law.
57. Providence itself could not be more absolutely improvident.
58. The public do not know enough to be experts, yet know enough to decide between them.
59. She is a very fascinating woman, and he is very fond of fascinating with her.
60. She looks as if her soul had got the better of her.
61. She ought never to have been a mother, but she'll make a rare mother-in-law.
62. She went up the Nile as far as the first crocodile.
63. The tendency of modern science is to reduce proof to absurdity by continually reducing absurdity to proof.

64. There is nothing so unthinkable as thought, unless it be the absence of thought.
65. There should be asylums for habitual teetotallers, but they would probably relapse into teetotalism as soon as they came out.
66. There should be some schools called deformatories to which people are sent if they are too good to be practical.
67. This age will serve to make a very pretty farce for the next.
68. 'Tis better to have loved and lost than never to have lost at all.
69. To live is like to love—all reason is against it, and all healthy instinct for it.
70. To the lexicographer, God is simply the word that comes next to 'go-cart'.
71. Two are better than one, but the man who said that did not know my sisters.
72. Vaccination is the medical sacrament corresponding to baptism.
73. Vouchsafe, O Lord, to keep us this day without being found out.
74. We are all miscarriages, but some miscarry at three months after conception and some at a hundred years after birth.
75. We ought to have books teaching us not how to compose music but how to decompose it.
76. We should so use the next world that it should advance us in that which is before it.
77. What I want to write is songs without words—or music.
78. You can do very little with faith, but you can do nothing without it.

BYRON, George Gordon, Lord, 1788–1824, *English poet.*

1. After all, what is a lie? 'Tis but the truth in masquerade.
2. All tragedies are finished by death; all comedies are ended by a marriage.
3. Believe a woman or an epitaph, or any other thing that's false, before you trust in critics.
4. The earth has nothing like a she-epistle.
5. The English winter—ending in July, to recommence in August.

6. He learned the arts of riding, fencing, gunnery, and how to scale a fortress—or a nunnery.
7. He was the mildest-manner'd man that ever scuttled ship or cut a throat.
8. I hate to hunt down a tired metaphor.
9. I hope to merit Heaven by making earth a Hell.
10. I wish he would explain his explanation.
11. One of the pleasures of reading old letters is the knowledge that they need no answer.
12. Pleasure's a sin, and sometimes sin's a pleasure.
13. Since Eve ate apples, much depends on dinner.
14. Society is now one polished horde, form'd of two mighty tribes, the Bores and Bored.
15. There is a tide in the affairs of women which, taken at the flood, leads—God knows where.
16. There's naught, no doubt, so much the spirit calms as rum and true religion.
17. Though I love my country, I do not love my countrymen.
18. Though women are angels, yet wedlock's the devil.
19. 'Tis pleasant, sure, to see one's name in print; a book's a book, although there's nothing in't.
20. What men call gallantry, and gods adultery, is much more common where the climate's sultry.

CABANIS, Pierre Jean Georges, 1757–1808
French physician and philosophical writer.

Poetry and religion are the product of the smaller intestines.

CABELL, James Branch, 1879–1958, *American novelist.*

1. The optimist proclaims that we live in the best of all possible worlds, and the pessimist fears this is true.
2. The religion of Hell is patriotism, and the government is an enlightened democracy.

CAMERON, Simon, 1799–1889, *American politician.*

An honest politician is one who when he is bought will stay bought.

CAMPBELL, Patrick, born 1913, *English humorous writer.*

Whenever I have a bath, I make a list of the things I am going to need, and check it carefully before entering the water.

CANNING, George, 1770–1827

English statesman and prime minister.

1. Nothing is so fallacious as facts, except figures.
2. Save, save, oh, save me from the Candid friend.

CAPEK, Karel, 1890–1938

Czech journalist, playwright, and short-story writer.

If dogs could talk, perhaps we'd find it just as hard to get along with them as we do with people.

CARLYLE, Thomas, 1795–1881

Scotch essayist, historian, and biographer.

1. Experience is the best of schoolmasters, only the school fees are heavy.
2. Four thousand people cross London Bridge daily, mostly fools.
3. The greatest of faults, I should say, is to be conscious of none.
4. I do not hate him nearly as much as I fear I ought to.
5. If Jesus Christ were to come today, people would not even crucify Him. They would ask Him to dinner, and hear what He had to say, and make fun of it.
6. If you are ever in doubt as to whether or not you should kiss a pretty girl, always give her the benefit of the doubt.
7. Love is not altogether a delirium, yet it has many points in common therewith.
8. Make yourself an honest man and then you may be sure there is one rascal less in the world.
9. There is a great discovery still to be made in literature, that of paying literary men by the quantity they do not write.
10. Upwards of five hundred thousand two-legged animals without feathers lie around us, in horizontal positions, their heads all in nightcaps, and full of the foolishest dreams.
11. A well-written life is almost as rare as a well-spent one.

CARROLL, Lewis, 1832–1898

Pseudonym of Charles Lutwidge Dodgson, English writer and mathematician.

1. As large as life, and twice as natural.
2. 'If everybody minded their own business', the Duchess said in a hoarse growl, 'the world would go round a great deal faster than it does.'
3. It's a poor sort of memory that only works backwards.
4. That's the reason they're called lessons, because they lessen from day to day.

CATO, Marcus Porcius ('the Censor'), 234–149 B.C.

Roman statesman.

1. I can pardon everybody's mistakes except my own.
2. I had rather men should ask why no statue has been erected in my honour, than why one has.
3. It is a difficult matter, my fellow citizens, to argue with the belly, since it has no ears.
4. Wise men learn more from fools than fools from wise men.

CAVOUR, Benso di, 1810–1861, *Italian statesman.*

I have discovered the art of fooling diplomats; I speak the truth and they never believe me.

CERVANTES, Miguel de, 1547–1616, *Spanish author.*

1. All women are good—good for nothing, or good for something.
2. Between a woman's 'yes' and 'no', I would not venture to stick a pin.
3. Everyone is as God made him, and often a great deal worse.
4. I drink when there is an occasion, and sometimes when there is no occasion.
5. I never thrust my nose into other men's porridge. It is no bread and butter of mine.
6. The most difficult character in comedy is the fool, and he must be no fool who plays that part.
7. The rich widow cries with one eye and rejoices with the other.

8. When a man says, 'Get out of my house! What do you want with my wife?'—there's no answer to be made.

CHAMFORT, Nicholas, 1741–1794, *French wit and writer.*

1. Bachelors' wives and old maids' children are always perfect.
2. A beautiful woman is paradise for the eyes, hell for the soul, and purgatory for the purse.
3. Change in fashion is the tax which the industry of the poor levies on the vanity of the rich.
4. Fame: the advantage of being known to those who do not know us.
5. If a woman were on her way to her execution, she would demand a little time to put on make-up.
6. If it were not for the government, we should have nothing left to laugh at in France.
7. In France we leave unmolested those who set fire to the house, and persecute those who sound the alarm.
8. In love, everything is true, everything is false; it is the one subject on which one cannot express an absurdity.
9. A lover is a man who tries to be more amiable than it is possible for him to be.
10. The loves of some people are but the result of good suppers.
11. Many men and women enjoy popular esteem, not because they are known, but because they are not known.
12. Most contemporary books give the impression of having been manufactured in a day, out of books read the day before.
13. One would risk being disgusted if one saw politics, justice, and one's dinner in the making.
14. Paris is a city of gaieties and pleasures where four-fifths of the inhabitants die of grief.
15. The public! The public! How many fools does it take to make up a public?
16. Society is composed of two great classes: those who have more dinners than appetite, and those who have more appetite than dinners.
17. The success of many books is due to the affinity between the mediocrity of the author's ideas and those of the public.

18. There are more fools than wise men and even in the wise man himself there is more folly than wisdom.
19. There are well-dressed foolish ideas just as there are well-dressed fools.
20. The threat of a neglected cold is for doctors what the threat of purgatory is for priests—a gold mine.
21. 'Tis easier to make certain things legal than to make them legitimate.
22. A woman is like your shadow—follow her, she flies; fly from her, she follows.

CHAPMAN, George, 1559–1634, *English poet and dramatist.*

1. Flatterers look like friends, as wolves like dogs.
2. When a man dies, the last thing that moves is his heart; in a woman, her tongue.
3. Young men think old men are fools; but old men know young men are fools.

CHASE, Ilka, born 1905?, *American actress and author.*

1. America's best buy for a nickel is a telephone call to the right man.
2. George Moore unexpectedly pinched my behind; I felt rather honored that my behind should have drawn the attention of the great master of English prose.
3. He's all buttoned up in an impenetrable little coat of complacency.
4. When he said we were trying to make a fool of him, I could only murmur that the Creator had beat us to it.

CHEKHOV, Anton, 1860–1904
Russian writer of short stories, plays, and novels.

1. If you are afraid of loneliness do not marry.
2. A man and a woman marry because both of them don't know what to do with themselves.
3. The university brings out all abilities, including incapability.
4. What a lot of idiots there are among ladies; people have got so used to it that they no longer notice it.

5. When an actor has money, he doesn't send letters but telegrams.
6. A woman is fascinated not by art, but by the noise made by those who are in the art field.

CHESTERFIELD, Lord (4th Earl of), 1694–1773
English statesman and man of letters.

1. As fathers commonly go, it is seldom a misfortune to be fatherless; and considering the general run of sons, as seldom a misfortune to be childless.
2. He and I have been dead these two years, but we don't choose to have it known.
3. I am sure that, since I have had the full use of my reason, nobody has ever heard me laugh.
4. I look upon opera as a magic scene contrived to please the eyes and the ears at the expense of the understanding.
5. If a fool knows a secret, he tells it because he is a fool.
6. If people are unwilling to hear you, better it is to hold your tongue than them.
7. If the multitude ever deviate into the right, it is always for the wrong reason.
8. The less one has to do, the less time one finds to do it in.
9. The manner of a vulgar man has freedom without ease; the manner of a gentleman has ease without freedom.
10. Most people enjoy the inferiority of their best friends.
11. Nature has hardly formed a woman ugly enough to be insensible to flattery upon her person.
12. The only solid and lasting peace between a man and his wife is doubtless a separation.
13. Our prejudices are our mistresses; reason is at best our wife, very often heard indeed, but seldom minded.
14. That silly, sanguine notion . . . that one Englishman can beat three Frenchmen, encourages, and has sometimes enabled, one Englishman, in reality, to beat two.
15. To govern mankind one must not overrate them.
16. Very ugly or very beautiful women should be flattered on their understanding, mediocre ones on their beauty.
17. We, my lords, may thank Heaven that we have something better than our brains to depend on.

18. Women's beauty, like men's wit, is generally fatal to the owners.

CHESTERTON, Gilbert Keith, 1874–1936
English journalist, author, and critic.

1. An adventure is only an inconvenience, rightly considered.
2. All our schools are finishing schools; they finish what has never been begun.
3. Art, like morality, consists in drawing the line somewhere.
4. The artistic temperament is a disease that afflicts amateurs.
5. The Bible tells us to love our neighbours, and also to love our enemies; probably because they are generally the same people.
6. Christianity has not been tried and found wanting; it has been found difficult and not tried.
7. Cocoa is a cad and coward. Cocoa is a vulgar beast.
8. Companionate marriage is so-called because the people involved are not married and will very rapidly cease to be companions.
9. The dipsomaniac and the abstainer both make the same mistake: they both regard wine as a drug and not as a drink.
10. The doctrine of human equality reposes on this: that there is no man really clever who has not found that he is stupid.
11. The earth is a place on which England is found.
12. The evolutionists seem to know everything about the missing link except the fact that it is missing.
13. Farce creates people who are so intellectually simple as to hide in packing cases or pretend to be their own aunts.
14. Free verse is like free love; it is a contradiction in terms.
15. The full potentialities of human fury cannot be reached until a friend of both parties tactfully intervenes.
16. The golden age only comes to men when they have, if only for a moment, forgotten gold.
17. Heaven sent us soda water as a torment for our crimes.
18. I believe in getting into hot water; it keeps you clean.
19. I don't care where the water goes if it doesn't get into the wine.

20. I do not believe in a fate that falls on men however they act; but I do believe in a fate that falls on them unless they act.
21. I gravely doubt whether women were ever married by capture; I think they pretended to be, as they do still.
22. I hate a quarrel because it interrupts an argument.
23. If a thing is worth doing, it is worth doing badly.
24. Inspiration at its best means breath, and only too frequently means wind.
25. It is a pity that people travel in foreign countries; it narrows their minds so much.
26. It is better to speak wisdom foolishly like the saints than to speak folly wisely like the deans.
27. A man knows what style of book he wants to write when he knows nothing else about it.
28. A man must be orthodox upon most things or he will never have time to preach his own heresy.
29. The men who really believe in themselves are all in lunatic asylums.
30. Merely having an open mind is nothing; the object of opening the mind, as of opening the mouth, is to shut it again on something solid.
31. The modern humanitarian can love all opinions, including the opinion that men are unlovable.
32. 'My country, right or wrong' is like saying, 'My mother, drunk or sober'.
33. The old religionists tortured men physically for a moral truth; the new realists torture men morally for a physical truth.
34. Once men sang together round a table in chorus; now one man sings alone for the absurd reason that he can sing better.
35. The only way of catching a train I ever discovered is to miss the train before.
36. Optimism: the noble temptation to see too much in everything.
37. Our wisdom, whether expressed in public or private, belongs to the world, but our follies belong to those we love.

38. A puritan is a person who pours righteous indignation into the wrong things.
39. Science in the modern world has many uses; its chief use, however, is to provide long words to cover the errors of the rich.
40. Silence is the unbearable repartee.
41. Some men never feel small, but these are the few men who are.
42. The success of the marriage comes after the failure of the honeymoon.
43. There are only three things in the world that women do not understand, and they are Liberty, Equality, and Fraternity.
44. There is a great deal of difference between the eager man who wants to read a book and the tired man who wants a book to read.
45. There is nothing the matter with Americans except their ideals; the real American is all right; it is the ideal American who is all wrong.
46. There is only one thing that requires real courage to say, and that is a truism.
47. Thieves respect property; they merely wish the property to become their property that they may more perfectly respect it.
48. The two things that a healthy person hates most between heaven and hell are a woman who is not dignified and a man who is.
49. What a glorious garden of wonders the lights of Broadway would be to anyone lucky enough to be unable to read.
50. The wickedest work in this world is symbolized not by a wine glass, but by a looking-glass.
51. A yawn is a silent shout.
52. Youth is always too serious, and just now it is too serious about frivolity.

CHURCHILL, Charles, 1731–1764, *English satirist and poet.*
Prudent Dulness marked him for a mayor.

CHURCHILL, Winston, 1874–1965

English statesman, soldier, and historian.

1. In those days he was wiser than he is now; he used frequently to take my advice.
2. It is a socialist idea that making profits is a vice; I consider the real vice is making losses.
3. It saves a lot of trouble if, instead of having to earn money and save it, you can just go and borrow it.
4. Men occasionally stumble over the truth, but most of them pick themselves up and hurry off as if nothing had happened.
5. Russia is a riddle wrapped in a mystery inside an enigma.
6. Sir, we must beware of needless innovation, especially when guided by logic.
7. They are decided only to be undecided, resolved to be irresolute, adamant for drift, all-powerful for impotence.
8. They told me how Mr. Gladstone read Homer for fun, which I thought served him right.

CICERO, Marcus Tullius, 106–43 B.C.

Roman orator, statesman, and philosopher.

1. It is surprising that an augur can see an augury without smiling.
2. A lover of himself, without any rival.
3. There is no fortress so strong that money cannot take it.
4. There is no opinion so absurd but that some philosopher will express it.
5. When you have no basis for an argument, abuse the plaintiff.

CLARKE, James Freeman, 1810–1888

American clergyman and writer.

A politician thinks of the next election; a statesman, of the next generation.

CLARKE, John, 1639?, *English compiler.*

A scholar at court is an ass among apes.

CLAUDEL, Paul, 1868–1955

French diplomat, poet, and dramatist.

It is fortunate that diplomats have long noses since they usually cannot see beyond them.

CLEMENCEAU, Georges, 1841–1929

French statesman, premier, and author.

1. Everything I know I learned after I was thirty.
2. War is much too important a matter to be left to the generals.

CLOUGH, Hugh Arthur, 1819–1861, *English poet.*

Thou shalt not kill, but need not strive officiously to keep alive.

COBB, Irvin Shrewsbury, 1876–1944

American journalist, humorous short-story writer, and raconteur.

1. A capacity for self-pity is one of the last things that any woman surrenders.
2. Epitaph: a belated advertisement for a line of goods that has been permanently discontinued.
3. Every line in her face is the line of least resistance.
4. A good storyteller is a person who has a good memory and hopes other people haven't.
5. He has more kinfolk than a microbe.
6. His words were long enough to run in serials.
7. I couldn't write the things they publish now, with no beginning and no end, and a little incest in the middle.
8. I once knew a fellow who spoke a dialect with an accent.
9. I've just learned about his illness; let's hope it's nothing trivial.
10. Learn all the rules, every one of them, so that you will know how to break them.
11. Men are vain, but they won't mind women working so long as they get smaller salaries for the same job.
12. Middle age: when you begin to exchange your emotions for symptoms.
13. Save whatever is current at the moment, except currency.

14. What is a croquette but hash that has come to a head?
15. Why should a worm turn? It's probably just the same on the other side.
16. Women now insist on having all the prerogatives of the oak and all the perquisites of the clinging vine.
17. You couldn't tell if she was dressed for an opera or an operation.

COBBETT, William, 1762–1835

English essayist, politician, and agriculturist.

1. Free yourself from the slavery of tea and coffee and other slopkettle.
2. Nouns of number, or multitude, such as *Mob*, Parliament, Rabble, House of Commons, Regiment, Court of King's Bench, Den of Thieves, and the like.

COCTEAU, Jean, 1889–1963

French novelist, poet, and playwright.

1. The course of a river is almost always disapproved of by the source.
2. The eyes of the dead are closed gently; we also have to open gently the eyes of the living.
3. One does not blame an epoch; one congratulates oneself on not having belonged to it.
4. The speed of a runaway horse counts for nothing.
5. Tact consists in knowing how far we may go too far.
6. The worst tragedy for a poet is to be admired through being misunderstood.

COGAN, Thomas, 1545?–1607, *English physician.*

Drink wine and have the gout; drink none and have the gout.

COLBERT, Jean Baptiste, 1619–1683

French statesman and financial reformer.

The art of taxation consists in so plucking the goose as to obtain the largest amount of feathers with the least amount of hissing.

COLBY, Frank Moore, 1865–1925

American editor, essayist, and encyclopædist.

1. Never burn an uninteresting letter is the first rule of British aristocracy.
2. A 'new thinker', when studied closely, is merely a man who does not know what other people have thought.
3. Satire is a lonely and introspective occupation, for nobody can describe a fool to the life without much patient self-inspection.
4. Self-esteem is the most voluble of the emotions.
5. When a young American writer seems mad, it is usually because an old one drives him crazy.

COLERIDGE, Samuel Taylor, 1772–1834

English poet, literary critic, and philosopher.

1. Only the wise possess ideas; the greater part of mankind are possessed by them.
2. Plagiarists are always suspicious of being stolen from.
3. Some men are like musical glasses—to produce their finest tones you must keep them wet.
4. Swans sing before they die; 'twere no bad thing should certain persons die before they sing.
5. There are three classes of elderly women: first, that dear old soul; second, that old woman; third, that old witch.
6. Until you understand a writer's ignorance, presume yourself ignorant of his understanding.
7. You abuse snuff! Perhaps it is the final cause of the human nose.

COLLINS, John Churton, 1848–1908, *English literary critic.*

1. Half our mistakes in life arise from feeling where we ought to think, and thinking where we ought to feel.
2. In prosperity our friends know us; in adversity we know our friends.
3. The secret of success in life is known only to those who have not succeeded.
4. Suicide is the worst form of murder, because it leaves no opportunity for repentance.

5. There can be only one end to marriage without love, and that is love without marriage.
6. To profit from good advice requires more wisdom than to give it.
7. Truth is the object of philosophy, but not always of philosophers.
8. We make more enemies by what we say than friends by what we do.
9. The world, like an accomplished hostess, pays most attention to those whom it will soonest forget.

COLLINS, Mortimer, 1827–1876, *English poet and novelist.*

A man is as old as he's feeling, a woman as old as she looks.

COLMAN, George (the elder), 1732–1794
English dramatist.

What a pity it is that nobody knows how to manage a wife but a bachelor.

COLMAN, George (the younger), 1762–1836
English dramatist.

1. I have henceforth the privilege of adding to my name the honourable title of A double S.
2. Love and a cottage! Eh, Fanny! Ah, give me indifference and a coach and six!
3. There he comes, in a snail's trot.

COLTON, Charles Caleb, 1780–1832
English clergyman and epigrammatic writer.

1. Examinations are formidable even to the best prepared, for the greatest fool may ask more than the wisest man can answer.
2. Genius, in one respect, is like gold; numbers of persons are constantly writing about both, who have neither.
3. If you would be known, and not know, vegetate in a village; if you would know, and not be known, live in a city.
4. Law and equity are two things which God hath joined, but which man has put asunder.

5. Lawyers are the only civil delinquents whose judges must of necessity be chosen from themselves.
6. Many books require no thought from those who read them, and for a very simple reason—they made no such demand upon those who wrote them.
7. Many speak the truth when they say that they despise riches, but they mean the riches possessed by other men.
8. Marriage is a feast where the grace is sometimes better than the dinner.
9. Men will wrangle for religion; write for it; fight for it; die for it; anything but live for it.
10. Most of our misfortunes are more supportable than the comments of our friends upon them.
11. Never join with your friend when he abuses his horse or his wife, unless the one is about to be sold and the other to be buried.
12. Some read to think, these are rare; some to write, these are common; and some read to talk, and these form the great majority.
13. Some reputed saints that have been canonized ought to have been cannonaded.
14. Subtract from many modern poets all that may be found in Shakespeare, and trash will remain.
15. There are three difficulties in authorship: to write anything worth the publishing, to find honest men to publish it, and to get sensible men to read it.
16. When the million applaud, you ask yourself what harm you have done; when they censure you, what good.

CONGREVE, William, 1670–1729, *English dramatist.*

1. Every man plays the fool once in his life, but to marry is playing the fool all one's life long.
2. Exceeding good to keep a secret, for though she should tell, yet she is not to be believed.
3. I am always of the opinion with the learned, if they speak first.
4. I came upstairs into the world, for I was born in a cellar.
5. I confess freely to you, I could never look long upon a monkey without very mortifying reflections.

6. If I continue to endure you a little longer, I may by degrees dwindle into a wife.
7. In my conscience I believe the baggage loves me, for she never speaks well of me herself nor suffers anybody else to rail at me.
8. She has that everlasting rotation of tongue, that an echo must wait till she dies before it can catch her last words.
9. She herself makes her own faces, and each morning wears a new one.
10. She is chaste who was never asked the question.
11. Though marriage makes man and wife one flesh, it leaves them still two fools.
12. A wit should be no more sincere than a woman constant.
13. You are a woman: you must never speak what you think; your words must contradict your thoughts, but your actions may contradict your words.

CONRAD, Joseph, 1857–1924, *English novelist.*

1. As to honour—you know—it's a very fine mediaeval inheritance which women never got hold of. It wasn't theirs.
2. Being a woman is a terribly difficult trade, since it consists principally of dealing with men.
3. The belief in a supernatural source of evil is not necessary; men alone are quite capable of every wickedness.
4. Gossip is what no one claims to like but everybody enjoys.
5. I can't imagine a human being so hard up for something to do as to quarrel with me.
6. Neither his fellows, nor his gods, nor his passions will leave a man alone.

COOLIDGE, Calvin, 1872–1933
President of the United States.

1. The business of America is business.
2. I sometimes wish that people would put a little more emphasis upon the observance of the law than they do upon its enforcement.
3. If you don't say anything, you won't be called on to repeat it.

4. Patriotism is easy to understand in America; it means looking out for yourself by looking out for your country.

COPLEY, Anthony, 1567–1607?, *English poet.*

Poor men want meat for their stomachs, rich men stomachs for their meat.

COWARD, Noel, born 1899

English actor, composer, and playwright.

1. Alfred Lunt has his head in the clouds and his feet in the box office.
2. Be it ever so humbug, there's no place like home.
3. I suppose they'll give you the custody of the Daimler?
4. It doesn't matter how bold you are when the dangerous age is past.
5. Mad dogs and Englishmen go out in the mid-day sun.
6. My reputation's terrible, which comforts me a lot.

COWLEY, Hannah, 1743–1809, *English dramatist.*

What is woman? Only one of Nature's agreeable blunders.

COWPER, William, 1731–1800, *English poet.*

1. A fool must now and then be right by chance.
2. A life of ease is a difficult pursuit.
3. A noisy man is always in the right.
4. Our severest winter, commonly called the spring.
5. The parson knows enough who knows a duke.
6. A self-made man? Yes—and worships his creator.
7. There is a public mischief in your mirth.

CRANE, Stephen, 1871–1900, *American novelist.*

Every sin is the result of a collaboration.

CREIGHTON, Mandell, 1843–1901

English bishop and biographer.

No people do so much harm as those who go about doing good.

CROSLAND, Thomas Williams Hodgson, 1865–1924
English journalist.

Your proper child of Caledonia . . . is taken by all the world to be fifty per cent cleverer and pluckier and honester than the facts warrant.

DALI, Salvador, born 1904, *Spanish-American painter.*

I do not paint a portrait to look like the subject, rather does the person grow to look like his portrait.

DARROW, Clarence, 1857–1938, *American lawyer.*

1. Depressions may bring people closer to the church, but so do funerals.
2. The first half of our lives is ruined by our parents and the second half by our children.
3. I am a friend of the working-man, and I would rather be his friend than be one.
4. I am an agnostic; I do not pretend to know what many ignorant men are sure of.
5. I have suffered from being misunderstood, but I would have suffered a hell of a lot more if I had been understood.
6. I never wanted to see anybody die, but there are a few obituary notices I have read with pleasure.
7. If a man is happy in America it is considered he is doing something wrong.
8. My constitution was destroyed long ago; now I'm living under the bylaws.
9. Some day I hope to write a book where the royalties will pay for the copies I give away.
10. The trouble with law is lawyers.
11. When I was a boy I was told that anybody could become President; I'm beginning to believe it.

DARWIN, Charles, 1809–1882, *English scientist.*

I love fools' experiments; I am always making them.

DAVIES, Jack, born 1913
English script writer and film critic.

Running after women never hurt anybody—it's catching 'em that does the damage.

DAVIES, William H., 1871–1940, *English poet and author.*

The more help a man has in his garden, the less it belongs to him.

DAVY, William, died 1780, *English lawyer.*

The farther I journey towards the West, the more convinced I am that the wise men came from the East.

DEEPING, Warwick, 1877–1950, *English novelist.*

1. He sat on the edge of his suspense.
2. He was a simple soul who had not been introduced to his own subconscious.
3. I spent a year in that town, one Sunday.

DEFFAND, Madame du, 1697–1780
French wit and letter writer.

Women are never stronger than when they arm themselves with their weakness.

DELAVIGNE, Casimir, 1793–1843
French poet and playwright.

Ever since Adam fools have been in the majority.

DELONEY, Thomas, 1543?–1607?
English ballad writer and pamphleteer.

God sends meat and the devil sends cooks.

DEWAR, Lord Thomas Robert, 1864–1930
British distiller and raconteur.

1. Confessions may be good for the soul but they are bad for the reputation.
2. Four-fifths of the perjury in the world is expended on tombstones, women, and competitors.
3. A husband should tell his wife everything that he is sure she will find out, and before anyone else does.
4. If Adam came on earth again the only thing he would recognize would be the old jokes.
5. It is only the people with push who have a pull.
6. Judge a man not by his clothes, but by his wife's clothes.

7. Lions of society are tigers for publicity.
8. Love is an ocean of emotions, entirely surrounded by expenses.
9. Minds are like parachutes: they only function when open.
10. No wife can endure a gambling husband unless he is a steady winner.
11. Nothing deflates so fast as a punctured reputation.
12. The one thing that hurts more than paying an income tax is not having to pay an income tax.
13. The road to success is filled with women pushing their husbands along.

DIBDIN, Charles, 1745–1814
English dramatist and song writer.

For a soldier I listed, to grow great in fame, and be shot at for sixpence a day.

DICKENS, Charles, 1812–1870, *English novelist.*

1. According to the constitution of mermaids, so much as is not a woman must be a fish.
2. Anythin' for a quiet life, as the man said wen he took the sitivation at the lighthouse.
3. As good people's very scarce, what I says is, make the best of 'em.
4. Battledore and shuttlecock's a wery good game, vhen you a'n't the shuttlecock and two lawyers the battledores, in which case it gets too excitin'.
5. Bring in the bottled lightning, a clean tumbler, and a cork-screw.
6. Business first, pleasure afterward, as King Richard said when he stabbed the other king in the Tower, before he smothered the babies.
7. Charity begins at home, and justice begins next door.
8. Credit: a person who can't pay, gets another person who can't pay, to guarantee that he can pay.
9. Do other men, for they would do you; that's the true business precept.
10. Every baby born into the world is a finer one than the last.

3

11. He'd be sharper than a serpent's tooth, if he wasn't as dull as ditchwater.
12. He'd make a lovely corpse.
13. He had but one eye, and the popular prejudice runs in favour of two.
14. He might have brought an action against his countenance for libel and recovered heavy damages.
15. I only know two sorts of boys. Mealy boys and beef-faced boys.
16. If a pig could give his mind to anything he would not be a pig.
17. If the law thinks it can make a woman do what she's made up her mind not to do, then the law is a bloomin' hass.
18. If there were no bad people, there would be no good lawyers.
19. In came a fiddler and tuned like fifty stomach-aches.
20. . . . in company with several other old ladies, of both sexes.
21. It is a melancholy truth that even great men have their poor relations.
22. It's my old girl that advises. She has the head. But I never own it before her. Discipline must be maintained.
23. Mr. Wopsle's great-aunt conquered a confirmed habit of living into which she had fallen.
24. A poor good-natur'd mean-spirited creetur as went out fishing for a wife one day, and caught a Tartar.
25. Regrets are the natural property of gray hairs.
26. She still aims at youth, though she shot beyond it years ago.
27. There are books of which the backs and covers are by far the best parts.
28. There are only two styles of portrait painting: the serious and the smirk.
29. Tongue; well that's a wery good thing when it ain't a woman's.
30. The virtues of mothers shall occasionally be visited upon the children, as well as the sins of the fathers.
31. Wery glad to see you, indeed, and hope our acquaintance may be a long 'un, as the gen'l'm'n said to the fi' pun note.

32. What is the odds so long as the fire of souls is kindled at the taper of conviviality, and the wing of friendship never moults a feather?
33. With affection beaming in one eye and calculation out of the other.
34. The words she spoke of Mrs. Harris, lambs could not forgive . . . nor worms forget.

DIDEROT, Denis, 1713–1784
French philosopher, critic, and encyclopædist.
The best doctor is the one you run for and can't find.

DISRAELI, Benjamin, 1804–1881
English statesman, novelist, and prime minister.
1. The author who speaks about his own books is almost as bad as the mother who talks about her own children.
2. The best way to become acquainted with a subject is to write a book about it.
3. The disappointment of manhood succeeds to the delusion of youth.
4. Every man has a right to be conceited until he is successful.
5. I have always thought that every woman should marry, and no man.
6. He has not a single redeeming defect.
7. He was distinguished for ignorance; for he had only one idea and that was wrong.
8. He was not an intellectual Croesus, but his pockets were full of sixpences.
9. I am bound to furnish my antagonists with arguments, but not with comprehension.
10. I never offered an opinion till I was sixty . . . and then it was one which had been in our family for a century.
11. If every man were straightforward in his opinions, there would be no conversation.
12. If you are not very clever, you should be conciliatory.
13. In politics, nothing is contemptible.
14. It is much easier to be critical than to be correct.
15. It is well known what a middleman is: he is a man who bamboozles one party and plunders the other.

16. It often happens that worthless people are merely people who are worth knowing.
17. The magic of first love is our ignorance that it can ever end.
18. A majority is always the best repartee.
19. My idea of an agreeable person is a person who agrees with me.
20. Plagiarists, at least, have the merit of preservation.
21. Romance has been elegantly defined as the offspring of fiction and love.
22. She is an excellent creature, but she never can remember which came first, the Greeks or the Romans.
23. A sophistical rhetorician, inebriated with the exuberance of his own verbosity.
24. Talk to a man about himself and he will listen for hours.
25. There are amusing people who do not interest, and interesting people who do not amuse.
26. There are three kinds of lies: lies, damned lies, and statistics.
27. When a man falls into his anecdotage, it is a sign for him to retire.
28. When I want to read a book I write one.
29. You know what a Toady is?—that agreeable animal which you meet every day in civilized society.
30. You know who critics are?—the men who have failed in literature and art.
31. Youth is a blunder, manhood a struggle, old age a regret.

D'ISRAELI, Isaac, 1766–1881
English compiler and commentator.
The defects of great men are the consolation of dunces.

DOBELL, Sydney Thompson, 1824–1874
English poet and critic.
As grand and griefless as a rich man's funeral.

DONNE, John, 1573–1631, *English poet and divine.*
For God's sake hold your tongue and let me love.

DOUGLAS, Norman, 1868–1952, *English author.*

1. Justice is too good for some people and not good enough for the rest.
2. Many a man who thinks to found a home discovers that he has merely opened a tavern for his friends.

DOYLE, Sir Arthur Conan, 1859–1930
English physician and novelist.

An experience of women which extends over many nations and three separate continents.

DRYDEN, John, 1631–1700, *English poet and dramatist.*

1. All heiresses are beautiful.
2. And thrice he routed all his foes, and thrice he slew the slain.
3. Here lies my wife: here let her lie. Now she's at rest, and so am I.
4. That unfeathered, two-legged thing, a son.

DUFFY, James, born 18—, *Irish dramatist.*

Thrifty! Man, she'd skin a flea for his hide.

DUKES, Ashley, 1885–1959, *English dramatist.*

1. I have noticed that the more pains men give themselves to shield a woman's name, the more widely her affairs are known.
2. The woman who runs will never lack followers.

DUMAS, Alexandre (père), 1803–1870
French novelist and dramatist.

1. The chain of wedlock is so heavy that it takes two to carry it, sometimes three.
2. Economy: the wealth of the poor and the wisdom of the rich.
3. I prefer the wicked rather than the foolish; the wicked sometimes rest.
4. It is often woman who inspires us with the great things that she will prevent us from accomplishing.

5. My father was a Creole, his father a Negro, and his father a monkey; my family, it seems, begins where yours left off.
6. We blame in others only the faults by which we do not profit.

DUMAS, Alexandre (fils), 1824–1895

French dramatist and novelist.

1. All generalizations are dangerous, even this one.
2. The Bible says that the last thing God made was woman; He must have made her on a Saturday night—it shows fatigue.
3. Business? It's quite simple; it's other people's money.
4. A husband is always a sensible man; he never thinks of marrying.

DUNNE, Finley Peter, 1867–1936

American humorist, creator of 'Mr. Dooley'.

1. The American nation in the sixth ward is a fine people; they love the eagle—on the back of a dollar.
2. Capital still pats Labor on the back—with an ax.
3. The Democratic Party ain't on speaking terms with itself.
4. I think if people marry it ought to be for life; the laws are altogether too lenient with them.
5. If a man is wise, he gets rich, and if he gets rich, he gets foolish, or his wife does.
6. If Christian Scientists had more science and doctors more Christianity, it wouldn't make any difference which you called in—if you had a good nurse.
7. A lie with a purpose is one of the worst kind, and the most profitable.
8. Life would not be worth living if we didn't keep our enemies.
9. A man never becomes an orator if he has anything to say.
10. Many a man that can't direct you to a corner drugstore will get a respectful hearing when age has further impaired his mind.
11. No matter whether the Constitution follows the flag or not, the Supreme Court follows the election returns.

12. One of the strangest things about life is that the poor, who need money the most, are the very ones that never have it.
13. The only good husbands stay bachelors; they're too considerate to get married.
14. The past always looks better than it was; it's only pleasant because it isn't here.
15. Theodore Roosevelt was president of the society of the first man up San Juan Hill.
16. There are no friends at cards or world politics.
17. Trust everybody, but cut the cards.
18. Vice is a creature of such hideous mien that the more you see it, the better you like it.
19. What's fame after all? 'Tis apt to be what someone writes on your tombstone.
20. The wise people are in New York because the foolish went there first; that's the way the wise men make a living.
21. Work is work if you're paid to do it, and it's pleasure if you pay to be allowed to do it.
22. You can refuse to love a man or to lend him money, but if he wants to fight you have got to oblige him.

D'URFEY, Thomas, 1653–1723, *English poet and dramatist.*

1. He has found a mare's nest and laughs at the eggs.
2. Take not the first refusal ill: tho' now she won't, anon she will.

EASTMAN, Max, 1883–1959, *American editor and writer.*

1. A poet in history is divine, but a poet in the next room is a joke.
2. Repartee is a duel fought with the points of jokes.

EDGEWORTH, Maria, 1767–1849, *English novelist.*

1. The bore is usually considered a harmless creature, or of that class of irrational bipeds who hurt only themselves.
2. Business was his aversion; pleasure was his business.

EDISON, Thomas Alva, 1847–1931, *American inventor.*

1. Everything comes to him who hustles while he waits.

2. Genius is one per cent inspiration and ninety-nine per cent perspiration.
3. When down in the mouth, remember Jonah: he came out all right.

EDWARDS, Oliver, 1711–1791

English solicitor and acquaintance of Dr. Johnson.

1. For my part, now, I consider supper as a turnpike through which one must pass, in order to get to bed.
2. I have tried in my time to be a philosopher; but, I don't know how, cheerfulness was always breaking in.

EINSTEIN, Albert, 1879–1955

German-American physicist, developed theory of relativity.

1. An empty stomach is not a good political adviser.
2. Isn't it strange that I who have written only unpopular books should be such a popular fellow?

ELDRIDGE, Paul, born 1888

American short-story writer, novelist, and poet.

1. Man is ready to die for an idea, provided that idea is not quite clear to him.
2. Many a crown of wisdom is but the golden chamberpot of success, worn with pompous dignity.
3. Many a necklace becomes a noose.
4. Never to have sinned is the unpardonable sin.
5. Reading the epitaphs, our only salvation lies in resurrecting the dead and burying the living.
6. There are those whose sole claim to profundity is the discovery of exceptions to rules.

ELIOT, George, 1819–1880

Pen-name of Mary Ann Evans, English novelist.

1. Animals are such agreeable friends; they ask no questions, they pass no criticisms.
2. An ass may bray a good while before he shakes the stars down.
3. Blessed is the man who, having nothing to say, abstains from giving wordy evidence of the fact.

4. The happiest women, like the happiest nations, have no history.
5. He's welly like a cock as thinks the sun's rose o' purpose to hear him crow.
6. Ignorance is not so damnable as humbug, but when it prescribes pills it may happen to do more harm.
7. I'm not denyin' the women are foolish; God Almighty made 'em to match the men.
8. I'm not one of those as can see the cat in the dairy, and wonder what she's come after.
9. I've never any pity for conceited people because I think they carry their comfort about with them.
10. It's hard work to tell which is Old Harry when everybody's got boots on.
11. She is like the rest of the women—thinks two and two'll come to make five, if she cries and bothers enough about it.
12. There is nothing will kill a man so soon as having nobody to find fault with but himself.
13. There isn't a thing . . . but what a man can do better than a woman, unless it's bearing children, and . . . it had better ha' been left to the men.

ELLIS, Havelock, 1859–1939, *English scientist and writer.*

1. Civilized men arrived in the Pacific, armed with alcohol, syphilis, trousers, and the Bible.
2. Heroes exterminate each other for the benefit of people who are not heroes.
3. The place where optimism most flourishes is the lunatic asylum.
4. A religion can no more afford to degrade its Devil than to degrade its God.
5. The self-styled decadent insists on lying down in the belief that he is hopelessly paralysed.
6. To be a leader of men one must turn one's back on men.
7. What we call 'Progress' is the exchange of one nuisance for another nuisance.
8. The whole religious complexion of the modern world is due to the absence from Jerusalem of a lunatic asylum.

EMERSON, Ralph Waldo, 1803–1882

American essayist, poet, and philosopher.

1. And what is a weed? A plant whose virtues have not been discovered.
2. Conversation is an art in which a man has all mankind for competitors.
3. Culture is one thing and varnish another.
4. Cunning egotism: if I cannot brag of knowing something, then I brag of not knowing it; at any rate, brag.
5. Democracy becomes a government of bullies tempered by editors.
6. Do what we can, summer will have its flies.
7. The end of the human race will be that it will eventually die of civilization.
8. Every hero becomes a bore at last.
9. Every man is an impossibility until he is born.
10. Every man is wanted, and no man is wanted much.
11. Every Stoic was a Stoic; but in Christendom, where is the Christian?
12. Fame is proof that the people are gullible.
13. Few envy the consideration enjoyed by the oldest inhabitant.
14. The first lesson of history is the good of evil.
15. A hero is no braver than an ordinary man, but he is brave five minutes longer.
16. If a man own land, the land owns him.
17. It is an amiable illusion, which the shape of our planet prompts, that every man is at the top of the world.
18. It is easy to live for others; everybody does.
19. Keep cool: it will be all one a hundred years hence.
20. Let us treat men and women well; treat them as if they were real; perhaps they are.
21. The louder he talked of his honor, the faster we counted our spoons.
22. A man of no conversation should smoke.
23. Many might go to heaven with half the labor they go to hell.
24. Men are conservative after dinner.
25. Men lose their tempers in defending their taste.

26. Men wish to be saved from the mischiefs of their vices, but not from their vices.
27. Money often costs too much.
28. My cow milks me.
29. Once we had wooden chalices and golden priests; now we have golden chalices and wooden priests.
30. People do not deserve to have good writing, they are so pleased with the bad.
31. The people are to be taken in very small doses.
32. A person seldom falls sick, but the bystanders are animated with a faint hope that he will die.
33. Society is a hospital of incurables.
34. The solar system has no anxiety about its reputation.
35. Speech is better than silence; silence is better than speech.
36. Take egotism out, and you would castrate the benefactors.
37. That which we call sin in others is experiment for us.
38. There is this benefit in brag, that the speaker is unconsciously expressing his own ideal.
39. Truth is beautiful without doubt, and so are lies.
40. We are always getting ready to live, but never living.
41. We do not count a man's years until he has nothing else to count.

ERVINE, St. John, born 1883

Irish playwright, novelist, and miscellaneous writer.

1. American motion pictures are written by the half-educated for the half-witted.
2. No one can fully appreciate the fatuity of human nature until he has spent some time in a box office.

FABRE, Jean Henri, 1823–1915, *French entomologist.*

History records the names of royal bastards, but cannot tell us the origin of wheat.

FADIMAN, Clifton, born 1904

American editor, writer, lecturer, and radio entertainer.

1. Born in a log cabin, Ambrose Bierce defied Alger's Law and did not become President.
2. Gertrude Stein is the mama of dada.
3. It is of such stuff and nonsense that dreams are made on.

FARQUHAR, George, 1678–1707, *English dramatist.*

1. Cupid is a blind gunner.
2. I don't think matrimony consistent with the liberty of the subject.
3. I see you have a singing face—a heavy, dull, sonata face.
4. There's no form of prayer in the liturgy against bad husbands.
5. 'Tis a strange . . . thing that among us people can't agree the whole week because they go different ways upon Sundays.
6. The tuneful serenade of that wakeful nightingale, his nose.
7. When the blind lead the blind, they both fall into—matrimony.

FÉNELON, François, 1651–1715, *French archbishop and writer.*

The more you say, the less people remember.

FERBER, Edna, 1887–1968

American novelist, short-story writer, and playwright.

Being an old maid is like death by drowning, a really delightful sensation after you cease to struggle.

FIELD, Eugene, 1850–1895

American journalist, poet, and humorist.

1. The actor who took the role of King Lear played the king as though he expected someone to play the ace.
2. Any color, so long as it's red, is the color that suits me best.
3. The biggest fish he ever caught were those that got away.
4. He is so mean, he won't let his little baby have more than one measle at a time.
5. The size of a woman's stomach depends largely on her surroundings.

FIELDING, Henry, 1707–1754, *English novelist.*

1. Beauty seldom recommends one woman to another.
2. Every physician almost hath his favourite disease.
3. His designs were strictly honourable, as the phrase is, that is, to rob a lady of her fortune by way of marriage.

4. How easy it is for man to die rich, if he will but be contented to live miserable.
5. Love and scandal are the best sweeteners of tea.
6. Money is the fruit of evil as often as the root of it.
7. Money will say more in one moment than the most eloquent lover can in years.
8. Some folks rail against other folks because other folks have what some folks would be glad of.
9. There's one fool at least in every married couple.
10. Thwackem was for doing justice and leaving mercy to heaven.
11. When children are doing nothing, they are doing mischief.
12. When widows exclaim loudly against second marriages, I would always lay a wager that the man, if not the wedding-day, is absolutely fixed-on.

FISCHER, Martin Henry, 1879–1962
American scientist, author, and educator.

1. The greatest discoveries of surgery are anesthesia, asepsis, and roentgenology—and none was discovered by a surgeon.
2. Half the modern drugs could well be thrown out the window, except that the birds might eat them.
3. I teach only the truth—but that shouldn't make you believe it.
4. Many a diabetic has stayed alive by stealing the bread denied him by his doctor.
5. The popular concept of a strengthening diet is a chicken wrung out in hot water.
6. We humans are greatest of the earth's parasites.

FISHBEIN, Morris, born 1889
American medical editor and writer.

He is an expert surgeon, brilliant pathologist, and an uncanny diagnostician, but he is somewhat rusty on advanced cigarette testimonials.

FITZGERALD, Percy, 1834–?, *Irish writer.*

She has eyes in the back of her head.

FLAMMARION, Camille, 1842–1925, *French astronomer.*

There are men who would even be afraid to commit themselves on the doctrine that castor oil is a laxative.

FLECKER, James Elroy, 1884–1915, *English poet and scholar.*

Thy impudence hath a monstrous beauty, like the hindquarters of an elephant.

FLORIO, John, 1553?–1625, *English translator and lexicographer.*

Who sleepeth with dogs shall rise with fleas.

FONTENELLE, Le Bovier de, 1657–1757, *French writer.*

1. A philosopher will not believe what he sees because he is too busy speculating about what he does not see.
2. There are three things I have always loved and never understood—art, music, and women.

FRANCE, Anatole, 1844–1924

Pen-name of Jacques Anatole Thibault, French novelist and critic.

1. The absurdity of a religious practice may be clearly demonstrated without lessening the number of persons who indulge in it.
2. The books that everybody admires are those that nobody reads.
3. Chance is the pseudonym of God when He did not want to sign.
4. Everything is not known but everything is said.
5. He despises men with tenderness.
6. History books which contain no lies are extremely dull.
7. If fifty million people say a foolish thing, it is still a foolish thing.
8. It is better to understand a little than to misunderstand a lot.
9. It is in the ability to deceive oneself that the greatest talent is shown.
10. The law, in its majestic equality, forbids the rich as well as the poor to sleep under bridges, to bed in the streets, and to steal bread.

11. Never lend books, for no one ever returns them; the only books I have in my library are books that other people have lent me.
12. Of all the ways of defining man, the worst is the one which makes him out to be a rational animal.
13. Only men who are not interested in women are interested in women's clothes; men who like women never notice what they wear.
14. People who have no faults are terrible; there is no way of taking advantage of them.
15. Religion has done love a great service by making it a sin.
16. There are very honest people who do not think that they have had a bargain unless they have cheated a merchant.
17. We do not know what to do with this short life, yet we want another which will be eternal.
18. We reproach people for talking about themselves; but it is the subject they treat best.
19. A woman must choose: with a man liked by women, she is not sure; with a man disliked by women, she is not happy.
20. A writer is rarely so well inspired as when he talks about himself.

FRANKLIN, Benjamin, 1706–1790

American statesman, author, scientist, inventor, and philosopher.

1. The absent are never without fault, nor the present without excuse.
2. All would live long, but none would be old.
3. Anger is never without a reason, but seldom with a good one.
4. Clean your finger before you point at my spots.
5. Clearly spoken, Mr. Fogg; you explain English by Greek.
6. Creditors have better memories than debtors.
7. The first mistake in public business is the going into it.
8. God heals, and the doctor takes the fee.
9. God works wonders now and then; behold, a lawyer, an honest man.
10. He's the best physician that knows the worthlessness of the most medicines.

11. He that falls in love with himself will have no rivals.
12. He that is good for making excuses is seldom good for anything else.
13. He that teaches himself hath a fool for a master.
14. He was so learned that he could name a horse in nine languages; so ignorant that he bought a cow to ride on.
15. Here comes the orator, with his flood of words and his drop of reason.
16. His conversation does not show the minute hand, but he strikes the hour very correctly.
17. If a man could have half his wishes, he would double his troubles.
18. If men are so wicked with religion, what would they be without it?
19. If you would keep a secret from an enemy, tell it not to a friend.
20. If you would know the value of money, go and try to borrow some.
21. If you would lose a troublesome visitor, lend him money.
22. If your riches are yours, why don't you take them with you to the other world?
23. An infallible remedy for toothache: wash the root of an aching tooth in vinegar, and let it dry half an hour in the sun.
24. Keep your eyes wide open before marriage, and half-shut afterwards.
25. The learned fool writes his nonsense in better language than the unlearned, but still 'tis nonsense.
26. Love your enemies, for they tell you your faults.
27. Love your neighbor, yet don't pull down your hedge.
28. Mankind are very odd creatures: one half censure what they practice, the other half practice what they censure.
29. Many a man would have been worse if his estate had been better.
30. Ne'er take a wife till thou hast a house (and a fire) to put her in.
31. Neither a fortress nor a maidenhead will hold out long after they begin to parley.
32. None preaches better than the ant, and she says nothing.

33. One good husband is worth two good wives; for the scarcer things are, the more they're valued.
34. Onions can make even heirs and widows weep.
35. The proud hate pride—in others.
36. Rich widows are the only secondhand goods that sell at first-class prices.
37. Samson with his strong body had a weak head, or he would not have laid it in a harlot's lap.
38. Savages we call them because their manners differ from ours.
39. She laughs at everything you say. Why? Because she has fine teeth.
40. Strange that a man who has wit enough to write a satire should have folly enough to publish it.
41. Teach your child to hold his tongue; he'll learn fast enough to speak.
42. There are more old drunkards than old doctors.
43. There are three faithful friends—an old wife, an old dog, and ready money.
44. There is much difference between imitating a good man and counterfeiting him.
45. Three may keep a secret if two of them are dead.
46. 'Tis against some men's principle to pay interest, and seems against other's interest to pay the principal.
47. To bear other people's afflictions, everyone has courage and enough to spare.
48. To find out a girl's faults, praise her to her girl friends.
49. What maintains one vice would bring up two children.

FRAZER, James George, 1854–1941, *Scottish anthropologist.*
Men make Gods, and women worship them.

FREDERICK the Great, 1712–1786, *King of Prussia.*
1. A German singer! I should as soon expect to get pleasure from the neighing of my horse.
2. If I wished to punish a province, I would have it governed by philosophers.
3. They say kings are made in the image of God; I feel sorry for God if that is what he looks like.

FROST, Robert, 1874–1963, *American poet.*

1. The best way out is always through.
2. The brain is a wonderful organ; it starts working the moment you get up in the morning, and does not stop until you get into the office.
3. By working faithfully eight hours a day, you may eventually get to be a boss and work twelve hours a day.
4. The difference between a man and his valet: they both smoke the same cigars, but only one pays for them.
5. A diplomat is a man who always remembers a woman's birthday but never remembers her age.
6. Half the world is composed of people who have something to say and can't, and the other half who have nothing to say and keep on saying it.
7. Home is the place where, when you have to go there, they have to take you in.
8. It's a funny thing that when a man hasn't got anything on earth to worry about, he goes off and gets married.
9. A jury consists of twelve persons chosen to decide who has the better lawyer.
10. A man will sometimes devote all his life to the development of one part of his body—the wishbone.
11. A mother takes twenty years to make a man of her boy, and another woman makes a fool of him in twenty minutes.
12. The reason why worry kills more people than work is that more people worry than work.
13. A receiver is appointed by the court to take what's left.
14. A successful lawsuit is the one worn by a policeman.
15. There is one thing more exasperating than a wife who can cook and won't, and that's the wife who can't cook and will.
16. Time and tide wait for no man, but time always stands still for a woman of thirty.
17. The world is full of willing people; some willing to work, the rest willing to let them.
18. Writing free verse is like playing tennis with the net down.

FULLER, Thomas, 1608–1661, *English physician and compiler.*

1. Age and wedlock we all desire and repent of.

2. Daughters and dead fish are no keeping wares.
3. The mob has many heads but no brains.
4. The road to ruin is always in good repair; the travellers pay the expense of it.
5. Silence is a fine jewel for a woman, but it's little worn.
6. Sorrow for a husband is like a pain in the elbow, short and sharp.
7. Wine hath drowned more men than the sea.
8. A women that paints puts up a bill that she is to let.
9. You make as good music as a wheelbarrow.

GALSWORTHY, John, 1867–1933
English novelist, playwright, and short-story writer.

1. For a man who can't see an inch into human nature, give me a psychological novelist.
2. The French cook; we open tins.
3. He's not worth my wiles.
4. I don't see the use in drawin' hard and fast rules. You only have to break 'em.
5. Idealism increases in direct proportion to one's distance from the problem.

GALTON, Francis, 1822–1911, *English scientist.*

Well-washed and well-combed domestic pets grow dull; they miss the stimulus of fleas.

GAUGUIN, Paul, 1848–1903, *French painter.*

Many excellent cooks are spoilt by going into the arts.

GAY, John, 1685–1732, *English poet and dramatist.*

1. The comfortable estate of widowhood is the only hope that keeps up a wife's spirits.
2. Do you think your mother and I should have lived comfortably so long together if ever we had been married?
3. I am ready, my dear Lucy, to give you satisfaction—if you think there is any in marriage.
4. An inconstant woman, tho' she has no chance to be very happy, can never be very unhappy.
5. Men were born to lie, and women to believe them.

6. Those who in quarrels interpose must often wipe a bloody nose.
7. Tho' I like your impudence, yet 'tis not so agreeable when put in practice against my wife.

GERALDY, Paul, born 1885, *French poet and playwright.*

1. As soon as you cannot keep anything from a woman, you love her.
2. Generally the woman chooses the man who will choose her.
3. It is well to love; not to love any more is well also.
4. Love is the effort a man makes to be satisfied with only one woman.
5. Women are not virtuous but they have given us the idea of virtue.
6. You leave your family for the sake of love to create another family which you may leave some day for another love.

GIBBON, Edward, 1737–1794, *English historian.*

1. The appellation of heretics has always been applied to the less numerous party.
2. Corruption, the most infallible symptom of constitutional liberty.
3. Dr. —— well remembered that he had a salary to receive, and only forgot that he had a duty to perform.
4. There is more pleasure in building castles in the air than on the ground.
5. To a philosophic eye the vices of the clergy are far less dangerous than their virtues.
6. Unprovided with original learning, unformed in the habits of thinking, unskilled in the arts of composition, I resolved—to write a book.

GIBBS, Philip, 1877–1962, *English journalist and novelist.*

It's better to give than to lend, and it costs about the same.

GIBBS, Wolcott, 1902–1958, *American writer and critic.*

He wasn't exactly hostile to facts but he was apathetic about them.

GIBRAN, Kahlil, 1883–1931, *Syrian-American poet and painter.*

An exaggeration is a truth that has lost its temper.

GIDE, André, 1869–1951

French critic, translator, and miscellaneous writer.

Art is a collaboration between God and the artist, and the less the artist does the better.

GILBERT, William Schwenck, 1836–1911

English humorous poet and playwright, collaborator in operas with Arthur Sullivan.

1. He did nothing in particular, and did it very well.
2. He led his regiment from behind. (He found it less exciting.)
3. In all the woes that curse our race, there is a lady in the case.
4. Isn't your life extremely flat with nothing whatever to grumble at?
5. It isn't so much what's on the table that matters, as what's on the chairs.
6. It is one of the happiest characteristics of this glowing country that official utterances are invariably regarded as unanswerable.
7. Life's perhaps the only riddle that we shrink from giving up.
8. Man is Nature's sole mistake.
9. No one can have a higher opinion of him than I have—and I think he is a dirty little beast.
10. Oh, don't the days seem lank and long, when all goes right and nothing goes wrong?
11. Perceptively intense and consummately utter. They are indeed jolly utter.
12. See how the Fates their gifts allot, for A is happy, B is not. Yet B is worthy, I dare say, of more prosperity than A.
13. She may very well pass for forty-three in the dusk with a light behind her.
14. You've no idea what a poor opinion I have of myself, and how little I deserve it.

GLASS, Montague, 1877–1934

English-American playwright and short-story writer.

She was a singer who had to take any note above A with her eyebrows.

GOETHE, Johann Wolfgang von, 1749–1832

German poet and dramatist.

1. Children, like dogs, have so sharp a scent that they detect everything—the bad before all the rest.
2. Everything in the world may be endured except continual prosperity.
3. I give presents to the mother, but I think of the daughter.
4. If children grew up according to early indications, we should have nothing but geniuses.
5. Of the best society it used to be said: its conversation affords instruction, but its silence imparts culture.
6. Some people spend the day in complaining of a headache, and the night in drinking the wine that gives it.
7. What must the English and French think of the language of our philosophers when we Germans do not understand it ourselves?

GOLDBERG, Isaac, 1887–1938

American critic, essayist, biographer, and short-story writer.

1. Diplomacy is to do and say the nastiest thing in the nicest way.
2. A gigolo is a fee-male.
3. The Good, the True, the Beautiful! Alas, the Good is so often untrue, the True so often unbeautiful, the Beautiful so often not good.
4. Grammar school never taught me anything about grammar.
5. I do not believe today everything I believed yesterday; I wonder will I believe tomorrow everything I believe today.
6. We spend half our lives unlearning the follies transmitted to us by our parents, and the other half transmitting our own follies to our offspring.

GOLDSMITH, Oliver, 1728–1774

English poet, novelist, and playwright.

1. As for disappointing them, I should not so much mind; but I can't abide to disappoint myself.
2. At this every lady drew up her mouth as if going to pronounce the letter P.
3. Every absurdity has a champion to defend it.
4. He writes indexes to perfection.
5. I always get the better when I argue alone.
6. I find you are perfectly qualified for making converts, and so go help your mother to make the gooseberry pie.
7. People seldom improve when they have no model but themselves to copy.
8. Silence is become his mother tongue.
9. There is nothing so absurd or ridiculous that has not at some time been said by some philosopher.
10. The true use of speech is not so much to express our wants as to conceal them.

GONCOURT, Edmond de, 1822–1896

French author and artist.

Genius is the talent of a man who is dead.

GOURMONT, Remy de, 1858–1915

French novelist, critic, and philosopher.

1. Before undergoing a surgical operation arrange your temporal affairs—you may live.
2. For two thousand years Christianity has been telling us: life is death, death is life; it is high time to consult the dictionary.
3. God is not all that exists; God is all that does not exist.
4. Good books are irrefutable, and bad books refute themselves.
5. It happens in life, as in grammar, that the exceptions outnumber the rules.
6. Man begins by making love and ends by loving a woman; woman begins by loving a man and ends by loving love.
7. Man has made use of his intelligence; he invented stupidity.

8. Most men who run down women are only running down a certain woman.
9. Of all sexual aberrations, perhaps the most peculiar is chastity.
10. Property is necessary, but it is not necessary that it should remain forever in the same hands.
11. Religions revolve madly around sexual questions.
12. The terrible thing about the quest for truth is that you find it.
13. To know what everybody knows is to know nothing.
14. Very simple ideas lie within the reach only of complex minds.
15. The woman one loves always smells good.
16. A woman sometimes feels pity for the sorrows that she causes without remorse.
17. Women are like the gentlemen of Molière's time; they know everything without having learned anything.
18. Women still remember the first kiss after men have forgotten the last.

GUBBINS, Nathaniel, born 1893

English humorous writer and columnist.

1. In that part of the world which is called civilized there are only three places you can avoid women—the club, the monastery, and the grave.
2. When idle women squawk for something they always get it, so in practically no time the civilized world was crawling with cuddly little doggies.

GUEDALLA, Philip, 1889–1944

English biographer and historian.

1. Any stigma will do to beat a dogma.
2. Biography is a region bounded on the north by history, on the south by fiction, on the east by obituary, and on the west by tedium.
3. He gives thanks that Britons never will be Slavs.
4. He holds the mirror up to Nietzsche.
5. Henry James had three reigns: James I, James II, and the Old Pretender.

6. History repeats itself; historians repeat each other.
7. The twentieth century is only the nineteenth speaking with a slightly American accent.

GUNTHER, John, born 1901, *American journalist and author.*
The famous politician was trying to save both his faces.

HALDANE, John B. S., 1892–1964, *English scientist.*
1. Even the ugliest human exteriors may contain the most beautiful viscera.
2. I've never met a healthy person who worried much about his health, or a good person who worried much about his soul.

HALIBURTON, Thomas Chandler, 1796–1865
Canadian jurist and humorist, creator of 'Sam Slick'.
1. A college education shows a man how little other people know.
2. Every woman is wrong until she cries, and then she is right, instantly.
3. Some people have a perfect genius for doing nothing, and doing it assiduously.
4. The Spaniards have it that a buxom widow must be either married, buried, or shut up in a convent.
5. Time is like a woman and pigs; the more you want it to go, the more it won't.

HALIFAX, George Savile, Marquis of, 1633–1695
English statesman and essayist.
1. The best qualification of a prophet is to have a good memory.
2. By the time men are fit for company, they see the objections to it.
3. Education is what remains when we have forgotten all that we have been taught.
4. If the laws could speak for themselves, they would complain of the lawyers in the first place.
5. A man that should call everything by its right name, would hardly pass the streets without being knocked down as a common enemy.

6. Some men's hats are as easily blown away as their heads.
7. The struggling for knowledge hath a pleasure in it like that of wrestling with a fine woman.
8. There are hardly two creatures of a more differing species than the same man when pretending to a place and when in possession of it.
9. The vanity of teaching doth oft tempt a man to forget that he is a blockhead.
10. When the people contend for their liberty they seldom get anything by their victory but new masters.
11. A wife is to thank God her husband has faults; a husband without faults is a dangerous observer.

HALL, Robert, 1764–1831, *English Baptist minister.*

1. He married public virtue in his early days, but seemed forever afterwards to be quarrelling with his wife.
2. He might be a very clever man . . . but he laid so many books upon his head that his brains could not move.

HALSEY, Margaret, born 1910, *American writer.*

1. He must have had a magnificent build before his stomach went in for a career of its own.
2. His handshake ought not to be used except as a tourniquet.

HANKIN, St. John, 1869–1909, *English dramatist.*

1. A clergyman with no politics is never made a bishop.
2. I'm quite in favour of temperance propaganda, providing it doesn't unduly restrict the sale of intoxicating liquor.

HARDY, Thomas, 1840–1928, *English novelist and poet.*

1. Ethelberta breathed a sort of exclamation, not right out, but stealthily, like a parson's damn.
2. A good wife is good, but the best wife is not so good as no wife at all.
3. He became a very celebrated bankrupt two or three times.
4. He secreted mirth on all occasions for special discharge at popular parties.
5. He was as irrepressibly good-humoured under ghastly snubs as a parliamentary candidate on the hustings.

6. He would box the charity boys' ears . . . till they could hardly stand upright, and do other deeds of piety natural to the saintly inclined.
7. Nater requires her swearing at the regular times, or she's not herself; and unholy exclamations is a necessity of life.
8. . . . A singular framework of clothes with nothing of any consequence inside them.
9. That man's silence is wonderful to listen to.
10. . . . A tone which showed her to be that novelty among women—one who finished a thought before beginning the sentence which was to convey it.
11. War makes rattling good history: but Peace is poor reading.
12. What between the poor men I won't have and the rich men who won't have me, I stand as a pelican in the wilderness.

HARINGTON, Sir John, 1561–1612, *English satirical writer.*

It is better to love two too many than one too few.

HARRIS, Joel Chandler, 1848–1908

American writer, creator of 'Uncle Remus'.

1. Liquor talks mighty loud when it gets loose from the jug.
2. The rooster makes more racket than the hen that lays the egg.
3. Watch out when you're getting all you want; fattening hogs ain't in luck.

HAY, Ian, 1876–1952

Pen-name of John Hay Beith, Scottish novelist and dramatist.

Marriage is a ghastly public confession of a strictly private intention.

HAZLITT, William, 1778–1830

English critic, essayist, and lecturer.

1. Actors are the only honest hypocrites.
2. Discussing the characters and foibles of common friends is a great sweetener and cementer of friendship.
3. Fashion is gentility running away from vulgarity, and afraid of being overtaken.

4. The greatest offence against virtue is to speak ill of it.
5. He who comes up to his own idea of greatness must always have had a very low standard of it in his mind.
6. I like a friend the better for having faults that one can talk about.
7. If mankind had wished for what is right, they might have had it long ago.
8. If the world were good for nothing else, it is a fine subject for speculation.
9. It is better to be able neither to read nor write than to be able to do nothing else.
10. It is essential to the triumph of reform that it should never succeed.
11. It is well there is no one without a fault, for he would not have a friend in the world.
12. Of all eloquence a nickname is the most concise; of all arguments the most unanswerable.
13. Of all the branches of political economy, the human face is perhaps the best criterion of value.
14. Silence is one great art of conversation.
15. Some persons make promises for the pleasure of breaking them.
16. There are names written in her immortal scroll at which Fame blushes.
17. There is a division of labour, even in vice; some persons addict themselves to the speculation only, others to the practice.
18. There is nothing so pedantic as pretending not to be pedantic.
19. Those who are fond of setting things to rights have no great objection to seeing them wrong.
20. The vices are never so well employed as in combating one another.
21. We are not satisfied to be right, unless we can prove others to be quite wrong.

HEDYLUS, 255? B.C., *Greek epigrammatist.*

The daughter of limb-relaxing Bacchus and limb-relaxing Aphrodite is limb-relaxing Gout.

HEGEL, Georg Wilhelm Friedrich, 1770–1831

German philosopher.

1. The people are that part of the state which does not know what it wants.
2. We learn from history that we do not learn from history.

HEINE, Heinrich, 1797–1856

German poet, critic, wit, and miscellaneous writer.

1. As soon as Eve ate the apple of wisdom, she reached for the fig leaf; when a woman begins to think, her first thought is of a new dress.
2. A blaspheming Frenchman is a spectacle more pleasing to the Lord than a praying Englishman.
3. *De mortuis nil nisi bonum*; of the living speak nothing but evil.
4. God will forgive me; that's His business.
5. The Hanoverian squires are asses who can talk of nothing but horses.
6. I do not know if she was virtuous, but she was ugly, and with a woman that is half the battle.
7. I fell asleep reading a dull book, and I dreamt that I was reading on, so I awoke from sheer boredom.
8. I have never seen an ass who talked like a human being, but I have met many human beings who talked like asses.
9. I will not say that women have no character; rather, they have a new one every day.
10. If the Romans had been obliged to learn Latin, they would never have found time to conquer the world.
11. Money is the god of our time, and Rothschild is his prophet.
12. The music at a marriage procession always reminds me of the music of soldiers marching to battle.
13. One should forgive one's enemies, but not before they are hanged.
14. Ordinarily he was insane, but he had lucid moments when he was merely stupid.
15. She resembles the Venus de Milo: she is very old, has no teeth, and has white spots on her yellow skin.
16. Silence—a conversation with an Englishman.

HELPS, Sir Arthur, 1813–1875

English author and Clerk of the Privy Council.

1. The absence of humility in critics is something wonderful.
2. The greatest luxury of riches is, that they enable you to escape so much good advice.
3. Reading is sometimes an ingenious device for avoiding thought.
4. Those awful goddesses, Appearances, are to us what the Fates were to the Greeks.
5. What a blessing this smoking is! Perhaps the greatest discovery that we owe to America!
6. The worst use that can be made of success is to boast of it.

HENLEY, W. E., 1849–1903, *English poet and critic.*

Far in the stillness a cat languishes loudly.

HENDERSON, Leon, born 1895, *American economist.*

A little inflation is like a little pregnancy—it keeps on growing.

HENRY, O., 1862–1910

Pen-name of William Sydney Porter, American short-story writer.

1. Life is made up of sobs, sniffles, and smiles, with sniffles predominating.
2. A straw vote only shows which way the hot air blows.

HERBERT, Alan Patrick, born 1890

English journalist and writer.

A highbrow is the kind of person who looks at a sausage and thinks of Picasso.

HERBERT, George, 1593–1633, *English divine and poet.*

1. Compliments cost nothing, yet many pay dearly.
2. He that hath a head of wax must not walk in the sun.
3. He that hath no honey in his pot, let him have it in his mouth.
4. A lean compromise is better than a fat lawsuit.
5. A piece of a churchyard fits everybody.

HERFORD, Oliver, 1863–1935

American humorous writer and illustrator.

1. Actresses will happen in the best-regulated families.
2. Alas: early Victorian for *oh, hell.*
3. Bigamy is one way of avoiding the painful publicity of divorce and the expense of alimony.
4. Cat: a pygmy lion who loves mice, hates dogs, and patronizes human beings.
5. Charity is the sterilized milk of human kindness.
6. Darling: the popular form of address used in speaking to a person of the opposite sex whose name you cannot at the moment recall.
7. Detour: something that lengthens your mileage, diminishes your gas, and strengthens your vocabulary.
8. Dilettante: a philanderer who seduces the several arts and deserts each in turn for another.
9. Diplomacy: lying in state.
10. A hair in the head is worth two in the brush.
11. I don't recall your name, but your manners are familiar.
12. If some people got their rights they would complain of being deprived of their wrongs.
13. In one's old coterie may one sport the old pantry and vestry.
14. In the midst of life we are in Brooklyn.
15. It's a strong stomach that has no turning.
16. Jade: a semi-precious stone or a semi-precious woman.
17. Jehovah has always seemed to me the most fascinating character in all fiction.
18. Junk is anything that has outlived its usefulness.
19. Liar: one who tells an unpleasant truth.
20. Lisp: to call a spade a thpade.
21. Lots of people have matrimonial troubles and don't know it.
22. A man is known by the silence he keeps.
23. Manuscript: something submitted in haste and returned at leisure.
24. Many are called but few get up.
25. Modesty: the gentle art of enhancing your charm by pretending not to be aware of it.
26. Monaco is the centre of the spinning industry of the world.
27. Money makes the mayor go.

28. The more waist, the less speed.
29. My wife has a whim of iron.
30. No one knows the worth of woman's love till he sues for alienation.
31. Nothing succeeds like—failure.
32. Only the young die good.
33. People who live in glass houses should pull down the blinds.
34. Perhaps it was because Nero played the fiddle, they burned Rome.
35. A rolling stone gathers no moss, but it gains a certain polish.
36. A soft drink turneth away company.
37. Song: the licensed medium for bawling in public things too silly or sacred to be uttered in ordinary speech.
38. There are more fish taken out of a stream than ever were in it.
39. There is no time like the pleasant.
40. There's always room at the top—after the investigation.
41. There's none so blind as those who won't fee.
42. What can't be cured must be insured.
43. What is my loftiest ambition? I've always wanted to throw an egg into an electric fan.
44. A woman's mind is cleaner than a man's; she changes it more often.
45. Zoo: a place devised for animals to study the habits of human beings.

HERODOTUS, 484?–425 B.C., *Greek historian.*

Very few things happen at the right time, and the rest do not happen at all; the conscientious historian will correct these defects.

HEROLD, Don, 1889–1966

American humorous writer and artist.

1. Be good, even at the cost of your self-respect.
2. Be kind and considerate to others, depending somewhat upon who they are
3. Be kind to dumb people.

4. The brighter you are, the more you have to learn.
5. Conversation is the slowest form of human communication.
6. Doctors know what you tell them.
7. Everything in life is fairly simple except one's wife.
8. Genius is an infinite capacity for giving pains.
9. Gentlemen prefer blondes, but take what they can get.
10. I say banish bridge; let's find some pleasanter way of being miserable together.
11. I wish I were either rich enough or poor enough to do a lot of things that are impossible in my present comfortable circumstances.
12. It takes a lot of things to prove you are smart, but only one thing to prove you are ignorant.
13. A lot of women are getting alimony who don't earn it.
14. A man can't have his soul and save it too.
15. Many people have character who have nothing else.
16. Marriage is a mistake of youth—which we should all make.
17. Married men live longer than single men, or at least they complain more about it.
18. Methods of locomotion have improved greatly in recent years, but places to go remain about the same.
19. 'The more articulate, the less said' is an old Chinese proverb which I just made up myself.
20. Oh, what a tangled web we weave when first we practice to conceive.
21. Poverty must have many satisfactions, else there would not be so many poor people.
22. Some people have had nothing else but experience.
23. There is nobody so irritating as somebody with less intelligence and more sense than we have.
24. There's one thing about baldness: it's neat.
25. We will hereafter believe less history than ever, now that we have seen how it is made.
26. When one has had to work so hard to get money, why should he impose on himself the further hardship of trying to save it?
27. Why resist temptation—there will always be more.
28. Women are not much, but they are the best other sex we have.

29. Women give us solace, but if it were not for women we should never need solace.
30. Women have a wonderful sense of right and wrong, but little sense of right and left.
31. Work is a form of nervousness.
32. Work is the greatest thing in the world, so we should always save some of it for tomorrow.

HIRSCHFELD, Magnus, 1868–1935, *German psychiatrist.*

Love is a conflict between reflexes and reflections.

HOBBES, Thomas, 1588–1679, *English philosopher.*

If I had read as much as other men, I should have known no more than other men.

HOLMES, Oliver Wendell, 1809–1894
American author, physician, and humorist.

1. All men are bores, except when we want them.
2. Apology is only egotism wrong side out.
3. The bore is the same eating dates under the cedars of Lebanon as over baked beans in Beacon Street.
4. Easy-crying widows take new husbands soonest; there's nothing like wet weather for transplanting.
5. Every library should try to be complete on something, if it were only the history of pinheads.
6. Everybody likes and respects self-made men; it's a great deal better to be made that way than not to be made at all.
7. Fate tried to conceal him by naming him Smith.
8. Give us the luxuries of life and we will dispense with necessaries.
9. Heredity is an omnibus in which all our ancestors ride, and every now and then one of them puts his head out and embarrasses us.
10. How many people live on the reputation of the reputation they might have made.
11. Humility is the first of the virtues—for other people.
12. I have always considered my face a convenience rather than an ornament.
13. Life is a fatal complaint, and an eminently contagious one.

14. Man has his will, but woman has her way.
15. Man wants but little here below, but wants that little strong.
16. The man who is always worrying whether or not his soul would be damned generally has a soul that isn't worth a damn.
17. Nature, when she invented, manufactured, and patented her authors, contrived to make critics out of the chips that were left.
18. One has to dismount from an idea and get into saddle again at every parenthesis.
19. Pink Tea: Giggle, Gabble, Gobble, Git.
20. Pretty much all the honest truth-telling there is in the world is done by children.
21. Self-abnegation is a rare virtue that good men preach and good women practice.
22. To be seventy years young is sometimes far more cheerful and hopeful than to be forty years old.
23. What I call a good patient is one who, having found a good physician, sticks to him till he dies.
24. Why can't somebody give us a list of things that everybody thinks and nobody says, and another list of things that everybody says and nobody thinks?

HOLYDAY, Barten, 1593–1661, *English divine and translator.*

A man may as well open an oyster without a knife as a lawyer's mouth without a fee.

HOOD, Thomas, 1799–1845, *English poet and humorist.*

1. Extremes meet, as the whiting said with its tail in its mouth.
2. Flatterers make cream cheese of chalk.
3. Holland lies so low, they're only saved by being damned.
4. Home-made dishes drive one from home.
5. I don't set up for being a cosmopolite, which to my mind signifies being polite to every country except your own.
6. One of the pleasures of having a rout is the pleasure of having it over.
7. There are three things which the public will always clamour for sooner or later, namely, novelty, novelty, novelty.

HOOK, Theodore, 1788–1841, *English novelist and wit.*
He used to cut his hair, but now his hair has cut him.

HOPE, Anthony, 1863–1933
Pen-name of Sir Anthony Hope Hawkins, English novelist and dramatist.

1. Economy is going without something you do want, in case you should some day want something which you probably won't want.
2. Good families are generally worse than others.
3. Telling the truth to people who misunderstand you is generally promoting a falsehood, isn't it?
4. Unless one is a genius, it is best to aim at being intelligible.
5. Your ignorance cramps my conversation.

HOPKINS, Gerard, born 1892, *English author and translator.*
At school a man finds his feet. At Oxford or at Cambridge he too often loses his balance.

HORACE, Quintus Horatius Flaccus, 65–8 B.C., *Latin poet.*

1. He prepares to go mad with fixed rule and method.
2. There is this vice in all singers, that if asked to sing among their friends they are never so inclined, but unasked they never leave off.

HOUSMAN, Alfred Edward, 1859–1936
English poet and classical scholar.
He drank like a fish, if drinking nothing but water could be so described.

HOUSSAYE, Arsène, 1815–1896
French writer of fiction, verse, criticism, and history.
A woman forgives only when she is in the wrong.

HOWE, Edgar Watson ('Ed'), 1853–1937
American journalist and author.

1. Half the world does not know how the other half lives, but is trying to find out.

2. If a loafer is not a nuisance to you, it is a sign that you are somewhat of a loafer yourself.
3. If you want to know how old a woman is, ask her sister-in-law.
4. Instead of loving your enemies, treat your friends a little better.
5. Men have as exaggerated an idea of their rights as women have of their wrongs.
6. One of the difficult tasks in this world is to convince a woman that even a bargain costs money.
7. One of the surprising things of this world is the respect a worthless man has for himself.

HOWELLS, William Dean, 1837–1920

American novelist, editor, critic, and miscellaneous prose writer.

Some people can stay longer in an hour than others can in a week.

HUBBARD, Elbert, 1856–1915

American author, editor, and printer.

1. Charity: a thing that begins at home, and usually stays there.
2. A conservative is a man who is too cowardly to fight and too fat to run.
3. Death: to stop sinning suddenly.
4. Do not take life too seriously; you will never get out of it alive.
5. Don't lose faith in humanity: think of all the people in the United States who have never played you a single nasty trick.
6. Editor: a person employed on a newspaper, whose business it is to separate the wheat from the chaff, and to see that the chaff is printed.
7. Every man is a damn fool for at least five minutes every day; wisdom consists in not exceeding the limit.
8. Every tyrant who has lived has believed in freedom—for himself.
9. Friend: one who knows all about you and loves you just the same.

10. Genius may have its limitations, but stupidity is not thus handicapped.
11. God: the John Doe of philosophy and religion.
12. The graveyards are full of people the world could not do without.
13. Heaven: the Coney Island of the Christian imagination.
14. Heaven is largely a matter of digestion.
15. If you don't advertise yourself you will be advertised by your loving enemies.
16. If you have no enemies, you are apt to be in the same predicament in regard to friends.
17. If you lose in an argument, you can still call your opponent names.
18. A man is as good as he has to be, and a woman as bad as she dares.
19. Man is Creation's masterpiece; but who says so?—Man.
20. Many a man's reputation would not know his character if they met on the street.
21. A miracle: an event described by those to whom it was told by men who did not see it.
22. No man needs a vacation so much as the person who has just had one.
23. The object of teaching a child is to enable him to get along without a teacher.
24. The only man who makes money following the races is the one who does so with a broom and shovel.
25. The path of civilization is paved with tin cans.
26. Perfume: any smell that is used to drown a worse one.
27. Repartee: any reply that is so clever that it makes the listener wish he had said it himself.
28. Righteous indignation: your own wrath as opposed to the shocking bad temper of others.
29. Secrets are things we give to others to keep for us.
30. Those whom God has put asunder no man can join together.
31. To avoid criticism, do nothing, say nothing, be nothing.
32. We are descended not only from monkeys, but from monks.

33. The world is moving so fast these days that the man who says it can't be done is generally interrupted by someone doing it.
34. Wrong no man and write no woman.
35. You can lead a boy to college but you cannot make him think.

HUBBARD, Frank McKinney ('Kin'), 1868–1930

American newspaper humorist and caricaturist, creator of 'Abe Martin'.

1. Boys will be boys, and so will a lot of middle-aged men.
2. Distant relatives are the best kind, and the further the better.
3. Every time I read where some woman gave a short talk I wonder how she stopped.
4. A friend that ain't in need is a friend indeed.
5. It's going to be fun to watch and see how long the meek can keep the earth after they inherit it.
6. It's pretty hard to tell what does bring happiness; poverty and wealth have both failed.
7. Many a family tree needs trimming.
8. Nobody works as hard for his money as the man who marries it.
9. Nobuddy ever fergits where he buried a hatchet.
10. One of the commonest ailments of the present day is premature formation of opinion.
11. The reason the way of the transgressor is hard is because it's so crowded.
12. The safest way to double your money is to fold it over once and put it in your pocket.
13. Some folks get credit for having horse sense that hain't ever had enough money to make fools of themselves.

HUGHES, Rupert, 1872–1956

American novelist, playwright, and editor.

1. Her face was her chaperone.
2. Love is a wonderful thing and highly desirable in marriage.
3. Women's intuition is the result of millions of years of not thinking.

HUGO, Victor, 1802–1885, *French poet, novelist, and dramatist.*

1. Everything bows to success, even grammar.
2. Forty is the old age of youth, fifty is the youth of old age.
3. God created the flirt as soon as He made the fool.
4. If you would civilize a man, begin with his grandmother.
5. Indigestion is charged by God with enforcing morality on the stomach.
6. Melancholy is the pleasure of being sad.
7. The peculiarity of prudery is to multiply sentinels in proportion as the fortress is less threatened.
8. Waterloo was a battle of the first rank won by a captain of the second.
9. When a woman is speaking to you, listen to what she says with her eyes.

HUME, David, 1711–1776, *Scottish historian and philosopher.*

I cannot but bless the memory of Julius Caesar, for the great esteem he expressed for fat men, and his aversion to lean ones.

HUNEKER, James Gibbons, 1860–1921
American editor, critic, and biographer.

1. Berlioz says nothing in his music, but he says it magnificently.
2. A critic is a man who expects miracles.
3. Do married men make the best husbands?
4. Every husband is my enemy.
5. Lawyers earn a living by the sweat of their browbeating.
6. Life is like an onion: you peel off layer after layer and then you find there is nothing in it.
7. My corns ache, I get gouty, and my prejudices swell like varicose veins.
8. When a woman writes her confessions she is never further from the truth.

HUXLEY, Aldous, 1894–1963
English novelist, essayist, and critic.

1. As the influence of religion declines, the social importance of art increases; we must beware of exchanging good religion for bad art.

2. A bad book is as much of a labour to write as a good one.
3. A bilious philosopher's opinion of the world can only be accepted with a pinch of salt, of Epsom salt by preference.
4. She was a professional athlete—of the tongue.
5. The silent bear no witness against themselves.
6. Technological progress has merely provided us with more efficient means for going backwards.
7. To his dog, every man is Napoleon; hence the constant popularity of dogs.
8. We are all geniuses up to the age of ten.

HUXLEY, Thomas Henry, 1825–1895, *English biologist.*

1. I have no faith, very little hope, and as much charity as I can afford.
2. If a little knowledge is dangerous, where is the man who has so much as to be out of danger?

IBSEN, Henrik, 1828–1906, *Norwegian dramatist and poet.*

1. It is inexcusable for scientists to torture animals; let them make their experiments on journalists and politicians.
2. You should never wear your best trousers when you go out to fight for freedom and truth.

INGE, William Ralph, 1860–1954
Anglican prelate and writer.

1. Even the paradise of fools is not an unpleasant abode while it is habitable.
2. Gaming is a disease of barbarians superficially civilized.
3. I am afraid the clergyman's God is too often the head of the clerical profession.
4. I have never understood why it should be considered derogatory to the Creator to suppose that he has a sense of humour.
5. In dealing with Englishmen you can be sure of one thing only, that the logical solution will not be adopted.
6. It is becoming impossible for those who mix with their fellow men to believe that the grace of God is distributed denominationally.

7. It is not easy for Catholics and Protestants to lie in the same bed, unless both are asleep.
8. It is useless for the sheep to pass resolutions in favour of vegetarianism while the wolf remains of a different opinion.
9. It may be doubted whether nature intended the Englishman to be a money-making animal.
10. A man may build himself a throne of bayonets, but he cannot sit on it.
11. Originality is undetected plagiarism.
12. Politicians take no interest in eugenics because the unborn have no vote.
13. The proper time to influence the character of a child is about a hundred years before he is born.
14. Religion is caught, not taught.
15. There are two kinds of fools: one says, 'This is old, therefore it is good'; the other says, 'This is new, therefore it is better'.
16. The whole of nature . . . is a conjunction of the verb to eat, in the active and passive.
17. Worry is interest paid on trouble before it falls due.

INGERSOLL, Robert Green, 1833–1899

American lawyer, writer, and lecturer.

1. Above all things, keep clean; it is not necessary to be a pig in order to raise one.
2. The church has always been willing to swap off treasures in heaven for cash down.
3. An honest God is the noblest work of man.
4. Hope is the only universal liar who never loses his reputation for veracity.
5. If I had my way I'd make health catching instead of disease.
6. If I owe Smith ten dollars, and God forgives me, that doesn't pay Smith.
7. Many people think they have religion when they are merely troubled with dyspepsia.
8. A mule has neither pride of ancestry nor hope of posterity.
9. Religion has not civilized man, man has civilized religion.

10. Whenever a man lives by prayer you will find that he eats considerable besides.
11. With soap, baptism is a good thing.

IRVING, Washington, 1783–1859

American short-story writer and essayist.

1. I am always at a loss to know how much to believe of my own stories.
2. A sharp tongue is the only edged tool that grows keener with constant use.
3. Whenever a man's friends begin to compliment him about looking young, he may be sure that they think he is growing old.
4. Young lawyers attend the courts, not because they have business there but because they have no business anywhere else.

ITURBI, José, born 1895

Spanish-American pianist and conductor.

The only time you realize you have a reputation is when you're not living up to it.

JACKSON, Holbrook, 1874–1948

English journalist, editor, author, and bibliophile.

1. As soon as an idea is accepted it is time to reject it.
2. Be contented, when you have got all you want.
3. Fear of corrupting the mind of the younger generation is the loftiest form of cowardice.
4. In democracies, those who lead, follow; those who follow, lead.
5. Intuition is reason in a hurry.
6. A lie is that which you do not believe.
7. Man is a dog's ideal of what God should be.
8. Man is the only animal that can be a fool.
9. The marriage system created a new sport—adultery.
10. Only the rich preach content to the poor.
11. The poor are the only consistent altruists; they sell all that they have and give to the rich.
12. Sacrifice is a form of bargaining.

13. Suffer fools gladly; they may be right.
14. There are only two classes in society; those who get more than they earn, and those who earn more than they get.
15. The typical man of any nation is the exception.
16. Why did Nature create man? Was it to show that she is big enough to make mistakes, or was it pure ignorance?

JAMES, Henry, 1843–1916, *Anglo-American novelist.*

1. For a man to pretend to understand women is bad manners; for him really to understand them is bad morals.
2. Life is a predicament which precedes death.
3. Naïveté in art is like zero in a number; its importance depends on the figure it is united with.

JAMES, William, 1842–1910
American psychologist and philosopher.

1. A great many people think they are thinking when they are merely rearranging their prejudices.
2. The obstinate insisting that Tweedledum is not Tweedledee is the bone and marrow of life.
3. When you have to make a choice and don't make it, that is in itself a choice.

JEFFERSON, Thomas, 1743–1826
American statesman and President of the United States.

1. Advertisements contain the only truths to be relied on in a newspaper.
2. It is the trade of lawyers to question everything, yield nothing, and to talk by the hour.
3. The man who reads nothing at all is better educated than the man who reads nothing but newspapers.

JEROME, Jerome K., 1859–1927
English humorous writer and novelist.

1. I like work; it fascinates me; I can sit and look at it for hours.
2. It is always the best policy to speak the truth, unless of course you are an exceptionally good liar.

3. It is impossible to enjoy idling thoroughly unless one has plenty of work to do.
4. Love is like the measles; we all have to go through it.
5. One of the advantages of being poor is that it necessitates the cultivation of the virtues.
6. We drink one another's healths and spoil our own.

JERROLD, Douglas, 1803–1857
English humorist, playwright, and editor.

1. The best thing I know between France and England is the sea.
2. Compared to the city, the country looks like the world without its clothes on.
3. A conservative is a man who will not look at the new moon, out of respect for that ancient institution, the old one.
4. Dogmatism is puppyism come to its full growth.
5. Earth is here so kind that, just tickle her with a hoe, and she laughs with a harvest.
6. Eve ate the apple that she might dress.
7. Every rose has its thorn: you never find a woman without pins and needles.
8. God said: 'Let us make man in our image'; and Man said: 'Let us make God in our image'.
9. The greatest animal in creation, the animal who cooks.
10. He is one of those wise philanthropists who, in a time of famine, would vote for nothing but a supply of toothpicks.
11. He should have an itch in the Temple of Fame.
12. He was so benevolent, so merciful a man that he would have held an umbrella over a duck in a shower of rain.
13. I've heard him renounce wine a hundred times a day, but then it has been between as many glasses.
14. If an earthquake were to engulf England tomorrow, the English would manage to meet and dine somewhere among the rubbish, just to celebrate the event.
15. If I were a gravedigger, or even a hangman, there are some people I could work for with a great deal of enjoyment.
16. In all the wedding cake, hope is the sweetest of the plums.
17. In marriage, as in war, it is permitted to take every advantage of the enemy.

18. In this world, truth can wait; she's used to it.
19. It seems so easy to be good-natured, I wonder anybody takes the trouble to be anything else.
20. A lady, being deserted by one man, has no other remedy than an appeal to twelve.
21. Love is like the measles—all the worse when it comes late in life.
22. Love the sea? I dote upon it—from the beach.
23. My notion of a wife at forty is that a man should be able to change her, like a bank note, for two twenties.
24. The only athletic sport I ever mastered was backgammon.
25. Readers are of two sorts: one who carefully goes through a book, and the other who as carefully lets the book go through him.
26. Self-defence is the clearest of all laws, and for this reason: the lawyers didn't make it.
27. The sharp employ the sharp; verily, a man may be known by his attorney.
28. The shirt of Nessus was a shirt not paid for.
29. Some people are so fond of ill luck that they run halfway to meet it.
30. A strange volume of real life in the packet of the postman. Eternal love and instant payment!
31. The surest way to hit a woman's heart is to take aim kneeling.
32. Talk to him of Jacob's ladder, and he would ask the number of the steps.
33. That fellow would vulgarize the Day of Judgment.
34. They say a parson first invented gunpowder, but one cannot believe it till one is married.
35. To reform a man is a tedious and uncertain labour; hanging is the sure work of a minute.
36. Troubles are like babies; they only grow by nursing.
37. Wedlock's like wine—not to be properly judged of till the second glass.
38. Whatever promises a man may make before marriage, the licence is as a receipt in full.
39. When a man has nothing in his cupboard, fever is his best guest.

40. Whenever a man exclaims that all mankind are villains, be assured that he contemplates an instant offer of himself as an exception.
41. With women as with warriors, there's no robbery—all's conquest.

JOAD, C. E. M., 1891–1953
English author and writer on philosophy.

When I was eleven, I thought that women were solid from the neck down.

JOHNSON, Samuel, 1709–1784
English author and lexicographer.

1. Abstinence is as easy to me as temperance would be difficult.
2. Adversity is the state in which a man most easily becomes acquainted with himself, being especially free from admirers then.
3. Criticism is a study by which men grow important and formidable at very small expense.
4. Every man has a right to utter what he thinks truth, and every other man has a right to knock him down for it.
5. The feeling of friendship is like that of being comfortably filled with roast beef; love, like being enlivened with champagne.
6. A fishing rod is a stick with a hook at one end and a fool at the other.
7. He is not only dull himself, but the cause of dullness in others.
8. He talks like a watch which ticks away minutes, but never strikes the hour.
9. He was dull in a new way, and that made many think him great.
10. I am very fond of the company of ladies; I like their beauty, I like their delicacy, I like their vivacity, and I like their silence.
11. I am willing to love all mankind, except an American.
12. I hate mankind, for I think myself one of the best of them, and I know how bad I am.

13. I live in the crowds of jollity, not so much to enjoy company as to shun myself.
14. I never take a nap after dinner but when I have had a bad night, and then the nap takes me.
15. I would be loth to speak ill of any person who I do not know deserves it, but I am afraid he is an attorney.
16. If he does really think that there is no distinction between vice and virtue, when he leaves our houses let us count our spoons.
17. In lapidary inscriptions a man is not upon oath.
18. The Irish are a fair people; they never speak well of one another.
19. It is better a man should be abused than forgotten.
20. Life is barren enough surely with all her trappings; let us be cautious therefore how we strip her.
21. A man in jail has more room, better food, and commonly better company.
22. A man is in general better pleased when he has a good dinner upon his table than when his wife talks Greek.
23. A man seldom thinks with more earnestness of anything than he does of his dinner.
24. Marriage has many pains, but celibacy has no pleasures.
25. Most schemes of political improvement are very laughable things.
26. Much may be made of a Scotchman, if he be caught young.
27. My diseases are an asthma and a dropsy and, what is less curable, seventy-five.
28. My idea of an agreeable person is one who agrees with me.
29. Nature has given women so much power that the law has very wisely given them little.
30. Network: anything reticulated or decussated at equal intervals with interstices between the intersections.
31. No human power can deprive the boaster of his own encomiums.
32. No man but a blockhead ever wrote except for money.
33. The noblest prospects which a Scotchman ever sees is the high road that leads him to England.
34. Nothing flatters a man as much as the happiness of his wife; he is always proud of himself as the source of it.

35. Nothing is more hopeless than a scheme of merriment.
36. Oats: a grain, which in England is generally given to horses, but in Scotland supports the people.
37. Of all noises I think music the léast disagreeable.
38. Patron: commonly a wretch who supports with insolence, and is paid with flattery.
39. The rights of nations and of kings sink into questions of grammar if grammarians discuss them.
40. Second marriage: the triumph of hope over experience.
41. That fellow seems to me to possess but one idea, and that a wrong one.
42. There are charms made only for distant admiration.
43. There is nothing too little for so little a creature as man.
44. Treating your adversary with respect is giving him an advantage to which he is not entitled.
45. We are inclined to believe those whom we do not know because they have never deceived us.
46. Were it not for imagination, a man would be as happy in the arms of a chambermaid as of a duchess.
47. What I gained by being in France was learning to be better satisfied with my own country.
48. What provokes your risibility, sir? Have I said something you can understand? Then I ask pardon for the rest of the company.
49. When a man knows he is to be hanged in a fortnight, it concentrates his mind wonderfully.
50. When a man says he had pleasure with a woman he does not mean conversation.
51. When two Englishmen meet, their first talk is of the weather.
52. Whoever thinks of going to bed before twelve o'clock is a scoundrel.
53. Wine makes a man better pleased with himself; I do not say that it makes him more pleasing to others.
54. A woman's preaching is like a dog's walking on his hind legs; it is not done well, but you are surprised to find it done at all.
55. Worth seeing? Yes, but not worth going to see.

56. You raise your voice when you should reinforce your argument.
57. You teach your daughters the diameters of the planets, and wonder what you have done that they do not delight in your company.
58. Your manuscript is both good and original; but the part that is good is not original, and the part that is original is not good.

JONES, Henry Arthur, 1851–1921, *English dramatist.*

1. It's a very useful and venerable superstition that one woman is perfectly safe if another woman is pretending to look after her.
2. Marriages are made in heaven, and if once we set to work to repair celestial mistakes and indiscretions, we shall have our hands full.
3. The one cruel fact about heroes is that they are made of flesh and blood.

JONSON, Ben, 1573?–1637, *English dramatist and poet.*

1. Man and wife make one fool.
2. Of all wild beasts preserve me from a tyrant; and of all tame a flatterer.

JOUBERT, Joseph, 1754–1824
French moralist and man of letters.

1. Children have more need of models than of critics.
2. It's better to debate a question without settling it than to settle a question without debating it.
3. We shall always keep a spare corner in our heads to give passing hospitality to our friends' opinions.
4. The whisper of a beautiful woman can be heard farther than the loudest call of duty.

JOWETT, Benjamin, 1817–1893
English Greek scholar and translator.

1. Even the youngest among us is not infallible.
2. Give the clergy your sympathy; don't give them anything else.

3. It is most important in this world to be pushing, but it is fatal to seem so.
4. Nowhere probably is there more true feeling, and nowhere worse taste, than in a churchyard.
5. The time he can spare from the adornment of his person he devotes to the neglect of his duties.

JUVENAL, Decimus Junius, *c.* 40–125 A.D.
Roman satirical poet.

1. The fisherman could perhaps be bought for less than the fish.
2. Give up all hope of peace so long as your mother-in-law is alive.

KARR, Alphonse, 1808–1890, *French editor and novelist.*

1. If men knew all that women think, they'd be twenty times more daring.
2. If we are to abolish the death penalty, I should like to see the first step taken by my friends the murderers.
3. Some people are always grumbling because roses have thorns; I am thankful that thorns have roses.
4. A woman who writes commits two sins: she increases the number of books, and decreases the number of women.

KIERKEGAARD, Sören Aabye, 1813–1855
Danish philosopher and writer on theology.

Life can only be understood backwards, but it must be lived forwards.

KINGSLEY, Charles, 1819–1875
English novelist, poet, and clergyman.

1. A keeper is only a poacher turned outside in, and a poacher a keeper turned inside out.
2. Love is sentimental measles.
3. There are more ways of killing a cat than choking her with cream.

KIPLING, Rudyard, 1865–1936
English poet, novelist, and short-story writer.

1. Adam was a gardener and God, who made him, sees that half of all good gardening is done upon the knees.

2. Borrow trouble for yourself, if that's your nature, but don't lend it to your neighbours.
3. Gardens are not made by singing 'Oh, how beautiful', and sitting in the shade.
4. He praised unblushingly her notes, for he was false as they.
5. Heaven grant us patience with a man in love!
6. Hit a man an' help a woman, an' ye can't be far wrong anyway.
7. I never made a mistake in my life; at least, never one that I couldn't explain away afterwards.
8. If the aunt of the vicar has never touched liquor, look out when she finds the champagne.
9. It's clever, but is it art?
10. Make 'im take 'er, an' keep 'er; that's hell for 'em both.
11. Man is an imperfectly denatured animal intermittently subject to the unpredictable reactions of an unlocated spiritual area.
12. Never praise a sister to a sister in the hope of your compliments reaching the proper ears.
13. She was as immutable as the hills, but not quite so green.
14. The silliest woman can manage a clever man, but it needs a very clever woman to manage a fool.
15. There's more things told than are true, and more things true than are told.
16. When the clergyman's daughter drinks nothing but water, she's certain to finish on gin.
17. A woman is only a woman, but a good cigar is a smoke.
18. A woman's guess is much more accurate than a man's certainty.
19. Youth had been a habit of hers for so long that she could not part with it.

KORZYBSKI, Alfred, 1879–1950, *American scientist and writer.*
God may forgive you your sins, but your nervous system won't.

KREISLER, Fritz, 1875–1962, *Austrian violinist and composer.*
In respect to violins, I am polygamous.

KRUTCH, Joseph Wood, born 1893
American critic and essayist.

There is no such thing as a dangerous woman; there are only susceptible men.

LA BRUYÈRE, Jean de, 1645–1696, *French writer and moralist.*

1. At the beginning of love and at its end, lovers are embarrassed if left alone.
2. The best way to get on in the world is to make people believe it's to their advantage to help you.
3. The court is like a palace built of marble, made up of very hard but very polished people.
4. The duty of a judge is to administer justice; but his practice is to delay it.
5. A fool is one whom bigger fools believe to be a man of merit.
6. It is a great misfortune neither to have enough wit to talk well nor enough judgment to be silent.
7. Next to good judgment, diamonds and pearls are the rarest things in the world.
8. The reason women do not love one another is—men.
9. There are no ugly women; there are only women who do not know how to look pretty.
10. There are only two ways of getting on in the world: by one's own industry, or by the stupidity of others.
11. Widows, like ripe fruit, drop easily from their perch.

LA FONTAINE, Jean de, 1621–1695
French poet and writer of fables.

1. It is difficult for a woman to keep a secret; and I know more than one man who is a woman.
2. It is impossible to please the whole world and your father as well.
3. This beast is very wicked; when it is attacked, it defends itself.
4. What is called discretion in men is called cunning in animals.

LAMARTINE, Alphonse de, 1790–1869
French poet, historian, statesman, and orator.

The more I see of the representatives of the people, the more I admire my dogs.

LAMB, Charles, 1775–1834, *English essayist and critic.*

1. Borrowers of books—those mutilators of collections, spoilers of the symmetry of shelves, and creators of odd volumes.
2. The first water cure was the Flood, and it killed more than it cured.
3. The greatest pleasure I know is to do a good action by stealth and have it found out by accident.
4. He did not stand shivering upon the brink, he was a thorough-paced liar, and plunged at once into the depths of your credulity.
5. He has left off reading altogether, to the great improvement of his originality.
6. He is no lawyer who cannot take two sides.
7. His life was formal; his actions seemed ruled with a ruler.
8. The human species is composed of two distinct races: the men who borrow, and the men who lend.
9. I am determined my children shall be brought up in their father's religion, if they can find out what it is.
10. I have been to a funeral; I can't describe to you the howl which the widow set up at proper intervals.
11. I have been trying all my life to like Scotchmen, and am obliged to desist from the experiment in despair.
12. I have not volition enough left to dot my i's, much less to comb my eyebrows.
13. I never knew an enemy to puns who was not an ill-natured man.
14. If dirt was trumps, what hands you would hold!
15. In everything that relates to science, I am a whole encyclopedia behind the rest of the world.
16. May my last breath be drawn through a pipe and exhaled in a pun.
17. A mixture of brandy and water spoils two good things.
18. My bedfellows are cough and cramp; we sleep three in a bed.
19. New Year's Day is every man's birthday.
20. Nothing is . . . more distasteful than that entire complacency and satisfaction which beam in the faces of a newly-married couple—in that of the lady particularly.

21. Nothing puzzles me more than time and space, and yet nothing puzzles me less, for I never think about them.
22. A poor relation is the most irrelevant thing in Nature.
23. Positively the best thing a man can have to do is nothing, and next to that, perhaps, good works.
24. Presents endear absents.
25. Satire does not look pretty upon a tombstone.
26. Sentimentally I am disposed to harmony; but organically I am incapable of a tune.
27. Since all the maids are good and lovable, from whence come the evil wives?
28. Tobacco has been my evening comfort and my morning curse.
29. The vices of some men are magnificent.
30. We read to say that we have read.
31. When my sonnet was rejected, I exclaimed: Damn the age; I will write for antiquity.
32. You look wise; pray, correct that error.

LANDON, Melville D. ('Eli Perkins'), 1839–1910

American humorous writer and lecturer.

1. A bore is a man who spends so much time talking about himself that you can't talk about yourself.
2. I hate the devil and I would kill him, but I see there are several clergymen present and they have their families to support.
3. Levity is the soul of wit.

LANDOR, Walter Savage, 1775–1864

English poet and prose writer.

1. I never did a single wise thing in the whole course of my existence, although I have written many which have been thought so.
2. Principles do not mainly influence even the principled; we talk on principle, but we act on interest.

LANG, Andrew, 1844–1912

Scottish poet, novelist, and scholar.

1. He missed an invaluable opportunity to hold his tongue.

2. He uses statistics as a drunken man uses lampposts—for support rather than for illumination.

LANGLAND, William, 1330?–1400?
English poet and author.

Adam, whiles he spake not, had paradise at will.

LARDNER, Ring, 1885–1933
American humorist and short-story writer.

1. He gave her a look that you could have poured on a waffle.
2. He looked at me as if I was a side dish he hadn't ordered.
3. It's the children's night out and I have to stay home with the nurse.
4. The only exercise I get is when I take the studs out of one shirt and put them in another.
5. An optimist is a girl who mistakes a bulge for a curve.
6. They gave each other a smile with a future in it.

LA ROCHEFOUCAULD, François de, 1613–1680
French epigrammatic writer.

1. Conceit causes more conversation than wit.
2. Everyone complains of his memory, no one of his judgment.
3. A fashionable woman is always in love with herself.
4. Gratitude is merely a secret hope of greater favours.
5. Greater qualities are necessary to bear good fortune than bad.
6. He who is pleased with nobody is much more unhappy than he with whom nobody is pleased.
7. Hypocrisy is the homage which vice pays to virtue.
8. If we did not flatter ourselves, the flattery of others would not harm us.
9. If we had no faults of our own, we should take less pleasure in noticing the faults of others.
10. If we judge love by most of its results, it resembles hatred rather than affection.
11. If we resist our passions, it is more from their weakness than from our strength.
12. In the misfortune of our best friends we find something which is not displeasing to us.

13. It is far better to be deceived than to be undeceived by those whom we love.
14. It is not always for virtue's sake that women are virtuous.
15. It takes much cleverness to know how to conceal cleverness.
16. The love of justice is, in most men, nothing more than the fear of suffering injustice.
17. A man who is always satisfied with himself is seldom satisfied with others.
18. Most of our faults are more pardonable than the means we use to conceal them.
19. Most virtuous women are like hidden treasures, safe only because they are not sought after.
20. Nothing prevents us from being natural so much as the desire to appear so.
21. Old men are fond of giving good advice to console themselves for their inability to give bad examples.
22. One can find women who have never had one love affair, but it is rare indeed to find any who have had only one.
23. Our enemies come nearer the truth in their opinions of us than we do in our opinion of ourselves.
24. People would not long remain in social life if they were not fooled by one another.
25. A person is never as happy or as unhappy as he thinks he is.
26. Philosophy triumphs easily over past and future misfortunes, but present misfortunes triumph over philosophy.
27. The reason lovers are never weary of each other is because they are always talking about themselves.
28. Repentance is not so much remorse for what we have done as the fear of consequences.
29. Solemnity is a trick of the body to hide the faults of the mind.
30. There are bad people who would be less dangerous if they had no good in them.
31. There are crimes which become innocent and even glorious through their splendour, number, and excess.
32. There are few people who are more often in the wrong than those who cannot endure to be thought so.
33. There are few people who are not ashamed of their love affairs when the infatuation is over.

34. There are few virtuous women who do not tire of their role.
35. There are people who would never have fallen in love if they had never heard of love.
36. There are some good marriages, but practically no delightful ones.
37. To establish oneself in the world, one does all one can to seem established there.
38. To love is the least of the faults of a loving woman.
39. To refuse praise is to seek praise twice.
40. True love is like a ghost: everybody talks about it but few have seen it.
41. Truth does not do so much good in the world as the appearance of it does evil.
42. Vanity is the greatest of all flatterers.
43. Virtue in women is often merely love of their reputation and of their peace of mind.
44. Virtue would not go far if vanity did not keep it company.
45. We all have enough strength to bear the misfortunes of others.
46. We always like those who admire us but we do not always like those whom we admire.
47. We are almost always bored in the company of persons with whom we are not permitted to be bored.
48. We are never made as ridiculous through the qualities we have as through those we pretend to.
49. We confess little faults in order to suggest that we have no big ones.
50. We give advice but we cannot give the wisdom to profit by it.
51. We give ourselves credit for the opposite faults of those we have: when we are weak, we boast of being obstinate.
52. We never confess our faults except through vanity.
53. We often do good in order that we may do evil with impunity.
54. We often forgive those who bore us, but we cannot forgive those whom we bore.
55. We often shed tears which deceive ourselves after deceiving others.

56. We prefer to speak evil of ourselves rather than not speak of ourselves at all.
57. We promise according to our hopes, and perform according to our fears.
58. We seldom find people ungrateful so long as we are in a condition to render them service.
59. We should have very little pleasure were we never to flatter ourselves.
60. We sometimes imagine we hate flattery, but we only hate the way we are flattered.
61. We think very few people sensible except those who agree with us.
62. We would often be ashamed of our best actions if the world only knew the motives behind them.
63. What is called liberality is often merely the vanity of giving.
64. What makes the vanity of other people intolerable is that it wounds our own.
65. What makes us so bitter against people who outwit us is that they think themselves cleverer than we are.
66. When our vices leave us, we flatter ourselves that we are leaving them.
67. Why can we remember the tiniest detail that has happened to us, and not remember how many times we have told it to the same persons?
68. Wit sometimes enables us to act rudely with impunity.
69. Women in love pardon great indiscretions more easily than little infidelities.
70. A woman is faithful to her first lover a long time—unless she happens to take a second.
71. You are never so easily fooled as when you are trying to fool someone else.

LAVATER, Johann Kaspar, 1741–1801

Swiss poet, mystic, and philosopher.

1. If you wish to appear agreeable in society you must consent to be taught many things which you already know.
2. Never say you know a man until you have divided an inheritance with him.

LAWRENCE, David Herbert ('D. H.'), 1885–1930
English novelist, poet, and essayist.

1. The unhappiness of a wife with a good husband is much more devastating than the unhappiness of a wife with a bad husband.
2. When I wish I was rich, then I know I am ill.

LEACOCK, Stephen, 1869–1944
Canadian political economist and humorist.

1. He flung himself upon his horse and rode madly off in all directions.
2. I am a great believer in luck, and I find the harder I work the more I have of it.
3. In a moment the pirates were all around us, rolling their eyes, gnashing their teeth, and filing their nails.
4. It's called political economy because it has nothing to do with either politics or economy.
5. Many a man in love with a dimple makes the mistake of marrying the whole girl.
6. Men are able to trust one another, knowing the exact degree of dishonesty they are entitled to expect.
7. The minute a man is convinced that he is interesting, he isn't.
8. The parent who could see his boy as he really is would shake his head and say, 'Willie is no good; I'll sell him'.

LEIGH, Henry Sambrooke, 1837–1883
English poet and dramatist.

The rapturous, wild and ineffable pleasure of drinking at somebody else's expense.

LEJEUNE, C. A., born 1897, ***English film critic.***

1. All the best whimsy puts sardines above caviare, sees heaven in a bed-sitting-room and stars in a puddle.
2. It does the bravest thing I have ever known a Hollywood film do—it admits that the people of America may be wrong.

3. The leading lady . . . modelled by a nearly new blonde with a personality; although it is perhaps a bit early to say whose.
4. . . . A scene that is all English and stiff upper lip. Nothing is said that can be regretted. Nothing is said that can even be remembered.
5. There are snake dancers . . . sacrifices . . . and a Holy Mountain. The mountain . . . has the privilege of belching when it is dissatisfied; something that the well-bred critic must not do.

LENCLOS, Ninon de, 1620–1705
French lady of fashion and wit.

1. Love never dies of starvation, but often of indigestion.
2. Men lose more conquests by their own awkwardness than by any virtue in the woman.
3. The resistance of a woman is not always a proof of her virtue, but more frequently of her experience.

LESSING, Gotthold, 1729–1781, *German critic and dramatist.*
A young lady who thinks is like a young man who rouges.

LEVANT, Oscar, born 1906
American pianist, composer, and wit.

1. An epigram is only a wisecrack that's played Carnegie Hall.
2. I've given up reading books; I find it takes my mind off myself.
3. In my last movie I played an unsympathetic character—myself.
4. The first thing I do in the morning is brush my teeth and sharpen my tongue.
5. My first wife divorced me on grounds of incompatibility, and besides, I think she hated me.
6. A pun is the lowest form of humor—when you don't think of it first.

LEWIS, George Henry, 1817–1878, *English writer.*
Murder, like talent, seems occasionally to run in families.

LICHTENBERG, Georg Christoph, 1742–1799

German physicist, satirist, and miscellaneous writer.

1. Everyone is a genius—at least once a year.
2. Language originated before philosophy, and that's what's wrong with philosophy.
3. What a blessing it would be if we could open and shut our ears as easily as we do our eyes.
4. What astonished him was that cats should have two holes cut in their skins at exactly the same places where their eyes were.
5. What if a man is buried alive from time to time? For every such person there are a hundred dead men walking the earth.

LINCOLN, Abraham, 1809–1865

President of the United States.

1. For people who like that kind of a book, that is the kind of a book they will like.
2. God must have loved the plain people; he made so many of them.
3. He can compress the most words into the smallest ideas of any man I ever met.
4. Honest statesmanship is the wise employment of individual meanness for the public good.
5. I don't know who my grandfather was; I am much more concerned to know what his grandson will be.
6. I fear explanations explanatory of things explained.
7. I was not accustomed to flattery; I was like the Hoosier who loved gingerbread better than any man and got less of it.
8. If this is coffee, please bring me some tea; but if this is tea, please bring me some coffee.
9. It has been my experience that folks who have no vices have very few virtues.
10. It's a good rule never to send a mouse to catch a skunk or a polliwog to tackle a whale.
11. Marriage is neither heaven nor hell, it is simply purgatory.
12. My father taught me to work; he did not teach me to love it.
13. My politics are short and sweet, like the old woman's dance.

14. No man has a good enough memory to make a successful liar.
15. The plainest print cannot be read through a gold eagle.
16. When I hear a man preach, I like to see him act as if he were fighting bees.
17. When you have got an elephant by the hind legs and he is trying to run away, it's best to let him run.
18. Whenever I hear anyone arguing for slavery, I feel a strong impulse to see it tried on him personally.

LINKLATER, Eric, born 1899, *Scottish novelist.*

America is the last abode of romance and other medieval phenomena.

LIN YUTANG, born 1895
Chinese philologist, essayist, and miscellaneous writer.

All women's dresses are merely variations on the eternal struggle between the admitted desire to dress and the unadmitted desire to undress.

LITTLE, Mary Wilson, born 1880?, *American paragrapher.*

1. Beauty in a woman's face, like sweetness in a woman's lips, is a matter of taste.
2. The bravest toreador in Spain would be nonplussed by an Irish bull.
3. He who devotes sixteen hours a day to hard study may become as wise at sixty as he thought himself at twenty.
4. If a man is only a little lower than the angels, the angels should reform.
5. If a mosquito bite thee on one hand, give him the other—palm downward.
6. In some parts of Ireland the sleep which knows no waking is always followed by a wake which knows no sleeping.
7. It is difficult to see why lace should be so expensive; it is mostly holes.
8. It is difficult to tell which gives some couples the most happiness, the minister who marries them or the judge who divorces them.
9. Men who make no pretensions to being good on one day out of seven are called sinners.

10. No man feels like laughing when he bumps his funny bone.
11. The only golden thing that women dislike is silence.
12. The penalty of success is to be bored by the attentions of people who formerly snubbed you.
13. Politeness is one half good nature and the other half good lying.
14. There is a great deal of prose licence in Walt Whitman's poetry.
15. There is no pleasure in having nothing to do; the fun is in having lots to do and not doing it.
16. The tombstone is about the only thing that can stand upright and lie on its face at the same time.
17. A youth with his first cigar makes himself sick; a youth with his first girl makes other people sick.

LLOYD GEORGE, David, 1863–1945
British statesman and prime minister.

A politician is a person with whose politics you don't agree; if you agree with him he is a statesman.

LOCKER-LAMPSON, Frederick, 1820–1895, *English poet.*

The world's as ugly, ay, as Sin—and almost as delightful.

LOCKIER, Francis, 1667–1740, *English divine and essayist.*

I never met with any one Scotchman but what was a man of sense . . . everybody of that country that has any leaves it as fast as they can.

LONGFELLOW, Henry Wadsworth, 1807–1882
American poet.

1. And so we plough along, as the fly said to the ox.
2. It takes less time to do a thing right than to explain why you did it wrong.

LOUIS XIV ('the Great'), 1638–1715, *King of France.*

1. Every time I fill a vacant office, I make ten malcontents and one ingrate.
2. I could sooner reconcile all Europe than two women.

LOVER, Samuel, 1797–1868

Irish novelist, portrait painter, and song writer.

When once the itch of literature comes over a man, nothing can cure it but the scratching of a pen.

LOWELL, James Russell, 1819–1891

American poet, editor, essayist, and diplomat.

1. Blessed are they who have nothing to say, and who cannot be persuaded to say it.
2. Democracy gives every man the right to be his own oppressor.
3. Don't ever prophesy—unless you know.
4. The foolish and the dead alone never change their opinions.
5. Granting our wish is one of Fate's saddest jokes.
6. He mastered whatever was not worth the knowing.
7. Let us be of good cheer, remembering that the misfortunes hardest to bear are those which never come.
8. There is no good in arguing with the inevitable; the only argument available with an east wind is to put on your overcoat.
9. What men prize most is a privilege, even if it be that of chief mourner at a funeral.
10. Whatever you may be sure of, be sure of this: that you are dreadfully like other people.

LUCAS, Edward Verrall, 1868–1938

English essayist and author.

1. The art of life is to be so well known at a good restaurant that you can pay with a cheque.
2. The best committee is a committee of two when one is absent.
3. I am a believer in punctuality though it makes me very lonely.
4. My desire, without any wish to make anybody's hair stand on end or flesh creep, is to call a spade a spade.
5. People who are late are often so much jollier than the people who have to wait for them.
6. The trouble with marriage is that, while every woman is at heart a mother, every man is at heart a bachelor.

LUTHER, Martin, 1483–1546
Leader of the Protestant Reformation in Germany.

1. If God consulted me I should have advised Him to continue the generation of the species by fashioning them of clay.
2. Who loves not women, wine and song remains a fool his whole life long.

LYLY, John, 1554?–1606, *English dramatist.*

1. Be sure always that your head be not higher than your hat.
2. Fish and guests in three days are stale.

LYTTON, Baron (Edward George Bulwer-Lytton), 1803–1873, *English novelist and dramatist.*

1. Castles in the air cost a vast deal to keep up.
2. A good cigar is as great a comfort to a man as a good cry to a woman.
3. If you wish to be loved, show more of your faults than your virtues.
4. It is difficult to say who do you the most mischief, enemies with the worst intentions, or friends with the best.
5. Just like my luck! If I had been bred a hatter, little boys would have come into the world without heads.
6. Life is like playing a violin solo in public and learning the instrument as one goes on.
7. Life would be tolerably agreeable if it were not for its amusements.
8. Love is the business of the idle, but the idleness of the busy.
9. A man who has ancestors is like a representative of the past.
10. There is no man so friendless but what he can find a friend sincere enough to tell him disagreeable truths.

MACAULAY, Rose, 1881–1958, *English novelist and essayist.*

1. Do not praise the ants' ready exsuscitation, but pity rather that entomological barrenness of invention which has never furnished this hard-worked insect with a really comfortable bed.
2. It was a book to kill time for those who like it better dead.

MACAULAY, Thomas Babington, Lord, 1800–1859

English historian, essayist, and poet.

1. An acre in Middlesex is better than a principality in Utopia.
2. Few of the many wise apothegms which have been uttered have prevented a single foolish action.
3. From Byron they drew a system of ethics in which the two great commandments were to hate your neighbour and to love your neighbour's wife.
4. His imagination resembled the wings of an ostrich. It enabled him to run, though not to soar.
5. It is possible to be below flattery, as well as above it.
6. Perhaps no person can be a poet, or even enjoy poetry, without a certain unsoundness of mind.
7. The Puritan hated bear-baiting, not because it gave pain to the bear but because it gave pleasure to the spectators.
8. Richard Steele was a rake among scholars, and a scholar among rakes.
9. We know of no spectacle so ridiculous as the British public in one of its periodical fits of morality.

MACDONNELL, A. G., 1903–1941

English journalist and humorous author.

1. Those whose lives are occupied in combating the eccentricities of God regard as very small beer the eccentricities of Man.
2. . . . The ups and downs to which Dame Fortune has seen fit in her inscrutable wisdom to subject us as a nation.

MACKENZIE, Compton, born 1883

English playwright and novelist.

Women do not find it difficult nowadays to behave like men, but they often find it extremely difficult to behave like gentlemen.

MADARIAGA, Salvador de, born 1886

Spanish diplomat and writer.

The Anglo-Saxon conscience does not prevent the Anglo-Saxon from sinning; it merely prevents him from enjoying his sin.

MAETERLINCK, Maurice, 1862–1949
Belgian poet, dramatist, and essayist.

1. All our knowledge merely helps us to die a more painful death than the animals that know nothing.
2. The living are the dead on holiday.

MAHAFFY, John Pentland, 1839–1919, *Irish scholar.*

Ireland is a country in which the probable never happens and the impossible always does.

MALLOCK, William H., 1849–1923, *English writer.*

Whatever may be God's future, we cannot forget His past.

MANN, Thomas, 1875–1955
German-American novelist and essayist.

A man's dying is more the survivors' affair than his own.

MANSFIELD, Katherine, 1888–1923
British short-story writer.

Regret is an appalling waste of energy; you can't build on it; it's only good for wallowing in.

MARQUIS, Don, 1878–1937, *American journalist and humorist.*

1. The females of all species are most dangerous when they appear to retreat.
2. Fishing is a delusion entirely surrounded by liars in old clothes.
3. He is so unlucky that he runs into accidents which started out to happen to somebody else.
4. He worked like hell in the country so he could live in the city, where he worked like hell so he could live in the country.
5. Hope is all right and so is Faith, but what I would like to see is a little Charity.
6. An idea isn't responsible for the people who believe in it.
7. If you make people think they're thinking, they'll love you; but if you really make them think, they'll hate you.

8. If you want to get rich from writing, write the sort of thing that's read by persons who move their lips when they're reading to themselves.
9. Mankind is being reformed, but conditions among the lower animals are frightful.
10. Middle age is the time when a man is always thinking that in a week or two he will feel as good as ever.
11. The more conscious a philosopher is of the weak spots of his theory, the more certain he is to speak with an air of final authority.
12. Most of the people living in New York have come here from the farm to try to make enough money to go back to the farm.
13. Ours is a world where people don't know what they want and are willing to go through hell to get it.
14. Procrastination is the art of keeping up with yesterday.
15. Publishing a volume of verse is like dropping a rose petal down the Grand Canyon and waiting for the echo.
16. The successful people are the ones who can think up things for the rest of the world to keep busy at.
17. There is always a comforting thought in time of trouble when it is not our trouble.
18. Young man, if she asks you if you like her hair that way, beware; the woman has already committed matrimony in her heart.

MARTIAL, A.D. 40?–102?, *Roman poet and epigrammatist.*

1. He does not write at all whose poems no man reads.
2. He was once a doctor but is now an undertaker; and what he does as an undertaker he used to do as a doctor.
3. If fame is to come only after death, I am in no hurry for it.
4. If you want him to mourn, you had best leave him nothing.
5. Lawyers are men who hire out their words and anger.
6. She has buried all her female friends; I wish she would make friends with my wife.
7. Such am I and you; but what I am you cannot be; but what you are anyone may be.

8. This is now the seventh wife that you have buried in your field; no one gets a better return from his field than you do.
9. The wife should be inferior to the husband; that is the only way to insure equality between the two.

MASEFIELD, John, 1878–1967
English poet, novelist, and dramatist.
His face was filled with broken commandments.

MASSON, Tom, 1866–1934, *American humorist and editor.*
1. After all, doesn't free love cost the most?
2. 'Be yourself!' is about the worst advice you can give to some people.
3. The best way to study human nature is when nobody else is present.
4. Hamlet is the tragedy of tackling a family problem too soon after college.
5. If Longfellow were alive today he would write: 'Sail on, thou Censorship of State'.
6. In modern wedlock, too many misplace the key.
7. It must be a hard life to be the child of a psychologist.
8. The love game is never called off on account of darkness.
9. No brain is stronger than its weakest think.
10. Professional charity—the milk of human blindness.
11. Prohibition may be a disputed theory, but none can complain that it doesn't hold water.
12. Reputation: what others are not thinking about you.
13. A senior always feels like the university is going to the kids.
14. Some girls never know just what they are going to do from one husband to another.
15. There are seventy million books in American libraries, but the one you want to read is always out.
16. Think of what would happen to us in America if there were no humorists; life would be one long Congressional Record.
17. To feel themselves in the presence of true greatness many men find it necessary only to be alone.

18. What if my trousers are shabby and worn; they cover a warm heart.
19. When billing and cooing results in matrimony, the billing always comes after the cooing.
20. You are not treating a girl right unless you ruin her digestion.
21. You can always get some one to love you—even if you have to do it yourself.

MAUGHAM, William Somerset, 1874–1965

English novelist, playwright, and short-story writer.

1. American women expect to find in their husbands a perfection that English women only hope to find in their butlers.
2. The degree of a nation's civilization is marked by its disregard for the necessities of existence.
3. England seems to me full of people doing things they don't want to do, because other people expect it of them.
4. Impropriety is the soul of wit.
5. In heaven when the blessed use the telephone they will say what they have to say and not a word besides.
6. It is a funny thing about life: if you refuse to accept anything but the best you very often get it.
7. Only a mediocre writer is always at his best.
8. To do each day two things one dislikes is a precept I have followed scrupulously: every day I have got up and I have gone to bed.
9. A woman can forgive a man for the harm he does her, but she can never forgive the sacrifices he makes on her account.
10. A woman will always sacrifice herself if you give her the opportunity. It is her favourite form of self-indulgence.

MAUROIS, André, 1885–1967

French biographer and miscellaneous writer.

1. The only thing experience teaches us is that experience teaches us nothing.
2. To have the licence number of one's automobile as low as possible is a social advantage in America.

3. A well-written life will always be rarer than a well-spent one.
4 When you become used to never being alone, you may consider yourself Americanized.

McFEE, William, 1881–1966, *Anglo-American writer.*
The world belongs to the Enthusiast who keeps cool.

MENCKEN, H. L., 1880–1956
American editor, critic, biographer, lexicographer, and satirist.

1. Adultery: democracy applied to love.
2. An anti-vivisectionist is one who gags at a guinea pig and swallows a baby.
3. Archbishop: a Christian ecclesiastic of a rank superior to that attained by Christ.
4. Bachelors know more about women than married men; if they didn't, they'd be married too.
5. The chief knowledge that a man gets from reading books is the knowledge that very few of them are worth reading.
6. Christian endeavour is notoriously hard on female pulchritude.
7. A church is a place in which gentlemen who have never been to heaven brag about it to persons who will never get there.
8. Clergyman: a ticket speculator outside the gates of heaven.
9. Conscience: the inner voice which warns us that someone may be looking.
10. A cow goes on giving milk all her life even though what appears to be her self-interest urges her to give gin.
11. A cynic is a man who, when he smells flowers, looks around for a coffin.
12. Democracy is also a form of religion; it is the worship of jackals by jackasses.
13. The difference between a moral man and a man of honour is that the latter regrets a discreditable act even when it has worked.
14. Don't overestimate the decency of the human race.
15. The dot is simply a bribe designed to overcome the disinclination of the male.

16. Every normal man must be tempted, at times, to spit on his hands, hoist the black flag, and begin slitting throats.
17. Faith may be defined briefly as an illogical belief in the occurrence of the improbable.
18. The first Rotarian was the first man to call John the Baptist Jack.
19. A gentleman is one who never strikes a woman without provocation.
20. Honeymoon: the time during which the bride believes the bridegroom's word of honour.
21. I go on working for the same reason that a hen goes on laying eggs.
22. In the main, there are two sorts of books: those that no one reads and those that no one ought to read.
23. In the United States, doing good has come to be, like patriotism, a favourite device of persons with something to sell.
24. In war the heroes always outnumber the soldiers ten to one.
25. Injustice is relatively easy to bear: what stings is justice.
26. It is a sin to believe evil of others, but it is seldom a mistake.
27. It is hard to believe that a man is telling the truth when you know that you would lie if you were in his place.
28. It is impossible to believe that the same God who permitted His own son to die a bachelor regards celibacy as an actual sin.
29. It was as necessary to me as honey to the bee or hell to the Christians.
30. A judge is a law student who marks his own examination papers.
31. Love is based on a view of women that is impossible to those who have had any experience with them.
32. Love is like war: easy to begin but very hard to stop.
33. Love is the delusion that one woman differs from another.
34. Love is the triumph of imagination over intelligence.
35. Man is always looking for someone to boast to; woman is always looking for a shoulder to put her head on.
36. Man weeps to think that he will die so soon; woman, that she was born so long ago.

37. Men have a much better time of it than women; for one thing, they marry later; for another thing, they die earlier.
38. The objection to Puritans is not that they try to make us think as they do, but that they try to make us do as they think.
39. The older I grow, the more I distrust the familiar doctrine that age brings wisdom.
40. On one issue at least, men and women agree: they both distrust women.
41. Opera in English is, in the main, just about as sensible as baseball in Italian.
42. The Parisians look forward to dinner as a Mississippian looks forward to his evening necking of the Scriptures.
43. The penalty for laughing in a courtroom is six months in jail; if it were not for this penalty, the jury would never hear the evidence.
44. Say what you will about the Ten Commandments, you must always come back to the pleasant fact that there are only ten of them.
45. A Sunday school is a prison in which children do penance for the evil conscience of their parents.
46. A teacher is one who, in his youth, admired teachers.
47. Theology is the effort to explain the unknowable in terms of the not worth knowing.
48. There is no record in human history of a happy philosopher.
49. 'Tis more blessed to give than to receive; for example, wedding presents.
50. The truth that survives is simply the lie that is pleasantest to believe.
51. The typical actor, at least in America, is the most upright of men; he always marries the girl.
52. When everyone begins to believe anything it ceases to be true; for example, the notion that the homeliest girl in the party is the safest.
53. When women kiss, it always reminds me of prize-fighters shaking hands.
54. Whenever a husband and wife begin to discuss their marriage, they are giving evidence at an inquest.

55. Wife: a former sweetheart.
56. A woman in love is less modest than a man; she has less to be ashamed of.
57. Women never acknowledge that they have fallen in love until the man has formally avowed his delusion and so cut off his retreat.

MEREDITH, George, 1828–1909, *English novelist and poet.*

1. After forty, men have married their habits, and wives are only an item in the list, and not the most important.
2. The future not being born, my friend, we will abstain from baptizing it.
3. In a dissension between a man and a wife, that one is in the right who has the most friends.
4. Kissing don't last: cookery do.
5. She poured a little social sewage into his ears.
6. She was a lady of incisive features bound in stale parchment.
7. Woman will be the last thing civilized by man.

MERRIMAN, Henry Seton, 1862–1903
Pseudonym of Hugh Stowell Scott, English novelist.

He was the product of an English public school and university . . . that is to say, he was no scholar but essentially a gentleman.

METTERNICH, Prince Von, 1773–1859
Austrian diplomat and statesman.

The English have better sense than any other nation—and they are fools.

MICHELET, Jules, 1798–1874, *French historian.*

How beautifully everything is arranged by Nature; as soon as a child enters the world, it finds a mother ready to take care of it.

MIKES, George, born 1913, *Anglo-Hungarian author and critic.*

1. English club life unites the liabilities of social life with the boredom of solitude.

2. A little foreign blood is very advantageous, almost essential, to become a really great British film producer.
3. On the Continent people have good food, in England people have good table manners.

MILNE, Alan Alexander, 1882–1956
English poet, playwright, and children's author.

No doubt Jack the Ripper excused himself on the grounds that it was human nature.

MIZNER, Addison, 1872–1933, *American architect.*

1. Absinthe makes the heart grow fonder.
2. Don't talk about yourself, it will be done when you leave.
3. Poets are born, not paid.
4. The poor ye have with ye always—but they are not invited.
5. Some people's genius lies in giving infinite pains.
6. A woman is never too old to yearn.
7. A woman on time is one in nine.

MIZNER, Wilson, 1876–1933
American dramatist, bon vivant, and wit.

1. Be nice to people on your way up because you'll meet them on your way down.
2. The best way to keep your friends is not to give them away.
3. I've had several years in Hollywood and I still think the movie heroes are in the audience.
4. Many a live wire would be a dead one except for his connections.
5. The most effective water power in the world—women's tears.
6. Most hard-boiled people are half-baked.
7. The only sure thing about luck is that it will change.
8. When a woman tells you her age, it's all right to look surprised, but don't scowl.

MOLEY, Raymond, born 1886
American journalist, editor, and political writer.

1. He walks as if balancing the family tree on his nose.
2. A political war is one in which everyone shoots from the lip.

MOLIÈRE, 1622–1673, *French actor and playwright.*

1. For more than forty years I have been speaking prose without knowing it.
2. I prefer a comfortable vice to a virtue that bores.
3. The only good thing about him is his cook, and the world visits his dinners and not him.
4. That must be wonderful; I don't understand it at all.

MONTAGU, Lady Mary Wortley, 1689–1762
English society leader and letter writer.

1. I despise the pleasure of pleasing people whom I despise.
2. I sometimes give myself admirable advice, but I am incapable of taking it.
3. If it was the fashion to go naked, the face would be hardly observed.
4. It goes far toward reconciling me to being a woman when I reflect that I am thus in no danger of marrying one.
5. When they tell me I have forsook the worship of my ancestors, I say I have had more ancestors heathen than Christian.

MONTAGUE, Charles Edward, 1867–1928
British journalist, essayist, and novelist.

War hath no fury like a noncombatant.

MONTAIGNE, Michel Eyquem de, 1533–1592
French essayist.

1. A doctor gets no pleasure out of the health of his friends.
2. Eloquence flourished most in Rome when public affairs were in the worst condition.
3. A good marriage would be between a blind wife and a deaf husband.
4. I don't remember ever having had the itch, and yet scratching is one of nature's sweet pleasures, and so handy.
5. If the world complains that I speak too much about myself, I complain that the world doesn't think of itself at all.
6. Is there anything so assured, resolved, disdainful, contemplative, solemn and serious as an ass?

7. It is easier to write a mediocre poem than to understand a good one.
8. Man is certainly stark mad: he cannot make a worm, and yet he makes gods by the dozen.
9. May God defend me from myself!
10. No one is exempt from talking nonsense; the misfortune is to do it solemnly.
11. Seeing she could not make fools wise, fortune has made them lucky.

MONTESQUIEU, Baron de, 1689–1755

French political philosopher and man of letters.

1. An author is a fool who, not content with having bored those who have lived with him, insists on boring future generations.
2. I have always observed that to succeed in the world one should seem a fool, but be wise.
3. If the triangles made a god, they would give him three sides.
4. What orators lack in depth they give you in length.
5. When God endowed human beings with brains, He did not intend to guarantee them.

MOORE, George, 1852–1933

Irish novelist, art critic, and essayist.

1. England produced Shakespeare; the British Empire the six-shilling novel.
2. Everybody sets out to do something, and everybody does something, but no one does what he sets out to do.
3. Faith goes out through the window when beauty comes in at the door.
4. Heaven may be for the laity, but this world is certainly for the clergy.
5. If good books did good, the world would have been converted long ago.
6. If there were no husbands, who would look after our mistresses?
7. In Ireland there is so little sense of compromise that a girl has to choose between perpetual adoration and perpetual pregnancy.

8. The incomparable stupidity of life teaches us to love our parents; divine philosophy teaches us to forgive them.
9. It is only with scent and silk and artifices that we raise love from an instinct to a passion.
10. The lot of critics is to be remembered by what they failed to understand.
11. Married folk know their bedfellows; bachelors, and perhaps spinsters, are never sure of theirs.
12. My one claim to originality among Irishmen is that I have never made a speech.
13. Nothing sharpens the wits like promiscuous flirtation.
14. People say you musn't love your friend's wife, but how are you to love your enemy's wife?
15. The poor would never be able to live at all if it weren't for the poor.
16. Remorse is beholding heaven and feeling hell.
17. Taking something from one man and making it worse is plagiarism.
18. There is always a right and a wrong way, and the wrong way always seems the more reasonable.
19. There is nothing so consoling as to find that one's neighbour's troubles are at least as great as one's own.
20. To be able to distinguish between a badly- and well-written book is not enough; a professor of literature can do that occasionally.
21. You must have women dressed, if it is only for the pleasure of imagining them as Venuses.

MOORE, Thomas, 1779–1852, *Irish poet.*

My only books were women's books, and folly's all they taught me.

MORLEY, Christopher, 1890–1957
American novelist, editor, and man of letters.

1. By the time the youngest children have learned to keep the place tidy, the oldest grandchildren are on hand to tear it to pieces again.

2. Dancing is wonderful training for girls; it's the first way you learn to guess what a man is going to do before he does it.
3. Few girls are as well shaped as a good horse.
4. God made man merely to hear some praise of what He'd done on those five days.
5. High heels were invented by a woman who had been kissed on the forehead.
6. A human being is an ingenious assembly of portable plumbing.
7. I hate to see men overdressed; a man ought to look like he's put together by accident, not added up on purpose.
8. If you have to keep reminding yourself of a thing, perhaps it isn't so.
9. Informal's what women always say they're going to be and never are.
10. Life is a foreign language: all men mispronounce it.
11. Lots of times you have to pretend to join a parade in which you're not really interested in order to get where you're going.
12. The most important autograph in a book is your own.
13. My theology, briefly, is that the universe was dictated but not signed.
14. No man is lonely while eating spaghetti—it requires so much attention.
15. Only the sinner has a right to preach.
16. The plural of spouse is spice.
17. Prophets were twice stoned: first in anger; then, after their death, with a handsome slab in the graveyard.
18. There are certain people whom one almost feels inclined to urge to hurry up and die so that their letters can be published.
19. There is only one rule for being a good talker: learn to listen.
20. There's so much to say but your eyes keep interrupting me.
21. Truth is not a diet but a condiment.
22. The war was not expurgated for those who went through it.
23. Your mind needs an uplift as well as your bust.

MORLEY, John, 1838–1923

English editor, biographer, and statesman..

1. Carlyle finally compressed his Gospel of Silence into thirty handsome octavos.
2. In politics the choice is constantly between two evils.
3. Letter-writing: that most delightful way of wasting time.
4. The proper memory for a politician is one that knows what to remember and what to forget.
5. Three things matter in a speech: who says it, how he says it, and what he says—and, of the three, the last matters the least.

MOSLEY, Leonard, born 1913, *English film critic.*

The air was damp with well-bred distress.

MUMFORD, Ethel Watts, 1878?–1940

American novelist and humorous writer.

1. Don't take the will for the deed; get the deed.
2. God gives us our relatives; thank God we can choose our friends.
3. In the midst of life we are in debt.
4. It is better to make friends fast than to make fast friends.
5. Knowledge is power, if you know it about the right person.
6. A man of courage never needs weapons, but he may need bail.
7. Oh wad some power the giftie gie us to see some people before they see us.
8. Think of your ancestors and your posterity, and you will never marry.
9. When folly is bliss, 'tis ignorance to be otherwise.

MURPHY, Arthur, 1727–1805, *English actor and dramatist.*

The people of England are never so happy as when you tell them they are ruined.

NAPOLEON BONAPARTE, 1769–1821

Emperor of the French.

1. Doctors will have more lives to answer for in the next world than even we generals.

2. I like convents, but I wish they wouldn't admit any women under the age of fifty.
3. Rascality has limits; stupidity has not.
4. Soldiers win battles and generals get the credit.
5. There are two kinds of fidelity, that of dogs and that of cats: you, gentlemen, have the fidelity of cats who never leave the house.

NASH, Ogden, 1902–1971, *American humorous poet.*

1. A little incompatibility is the spice of life, particularly if he has income and she is pattable.
2. Marriage is the alliance of two people, one of whom never remembers birthdays and the other never forgets them.
3. Marriage is the only known example of the happy meeting of the immovable object and the irresistible force.
4. Parents were invented to make children happy by giving them something to ignore.
5. The reason for much matrimony is patrimony.
6. Why did the Lord give us so much quickness of movement unless it was to avoid responsibility?

NATHAN, George Jean, 1882–1958
American editor, author, and dramatic critic.

1. Bad officials are elected by good citizens who do not vote.
2. He has ever been the tin can on his own tail.
3. He writes his plays for the ages—the ages between five and twelve.
4. Opening night: the night before the play is ready to open.
5. An optimist is a fellow who believes a housefly is looking for a way to get out.
6. What passes for woman's intuition is often nothing more than man's transparency.

NEVINSON, Henry W., 1856–1941
English newspaper correspondent and essayist.

Chivalry: going about releasing beautiful maidens from other men's castles, and taking them to your own castle.

NEWTON, Isaac, 1642–1727
English scientist and mathematician.

O physics! Preserve me from metaphysics!

NICHOLS, Beverley, born 1899, *English novelist and essayist.*

1. Marriage is a book of which the first chapter is written in poetry and the remaining chapters in prose.
2. When a woman is wearing shorts her charms are enlarged without being enhanced.
3. The worst thing you can possibly do to a woman is to deprive her of a grievance.

NICOLSON, Harold, 1886–1968, *English biographer and critic.*

The Irish do not want anyone to wish them well; they want everyone to wish their enemies ill.

NIETZSCHE, Friedrich Wilhelm, 1844–1900
German philosopher and writer.

1. Blessed are the forgetful, for they get the better even of their blunders.
2. A casual stroll through a lunatic asylum shows that faith does not prove anything.
3. Chastity is a virtue in some, but in many almost a vice.
4. The earth has a skin and that skin has diseases; one of its diseases is called man.
5. Even concubinage has been corrupted—by marriage.
6. He who cannot lie doesn't know what truth is.
7. I do not give alms; I am not poor enough for that.
8. I would believe only in a God that knows how to dance.
9. If a man really has strong faith he can indulge in the luxury of scepticism.
10. In the beginning was nonsense, and the nonsense was with God, and the nonsense was God.
11. The last Christian died on the cross.
12. Marriage makes an end of many short follies—being one long stupidity.
13. A married philosopher is necessarily comic.
14. Neighbours praise unselfishness because they profit by it.

15. No small art is it to sleep: it is necessary to keep awake all day for that purpose.
16. One should not go into churches if one wants to breathe pure air.
17. Some die too young, and some die too old, the precept sounds strange, but die at the right time.
18. There are two things a real man likes—danger and play; and he likes woman because she is the most dangerous of playthings.
19. There is not enough religion is the world even to destroy the world's religions.
20. We are most unfair to God: we do not allow Him to sin.
21. When a woman becomes a scholar there is usually something wrong with her sexual organs.
22. Which is it—is man one of God's blunders or is God one of man's blunders?
23. Woman was God's second mistake.

NOVALIS, 1772–1801
Pseudonym of Friedrich-Leopold von Hardenberg, German poet and novelist.
Not only England, but every Englishman is an island.

NYE, Edgar Wilson ('Bill'), 1850–1896, *American humorist.*
1. Be virtuous and you will be happy; but you will be lonesome, sometimes.
2. Many public speakers are good extemporaneous listeners.
3. Winter lingered so long in the lap of Spring that it occasioned a great deal of talk.

O'MALLEY, Austin, 1858–1932
American oculist and miscellaneous writer.
1. After thirty-five a man begins to have thoughts about women; before that age he has feelings.
2. All things come to him who waits—even justice.
3. The American government is a rule of the people, by the people, for the boss.
4. The best blood will at some time get into a fool or a mosquito.

5. The best part of a real-estate bargain is the neighbor.
6. The best throw of the dice is to throw them away.
7. Better a bald head than none at all.
8. Busy souls have no time to be busybodies.
9. Circumstantial evidence is like a blackberry, which when red or white is really green.
10. A drunkard is like a whisky bottle, all neck and belly and no head.
11. A dyspeptic is a man that can eat his cake and have it too.
12. An Englishman thinks seated; a Frenchman, standing; an American, pacing; an Irishman, afterward.
13. Exclusiveness is a characteristic of recent riches, high society, and the skunk.
14. A gentleman never heard the story before.
15. Gift is a synonym of trade.
16. God shows his contempt for wealth by the kind of person he selects to receive it.
17. A habit of debt is very injurious to the memory.
18. The half-baked sermon causes spiritual indigestion.
19. A hole is nothing at all, but you can break your neck in it.
20. If you keep your eyes so fixed on heaven that you never look at the earth, you will stumble into hell.
21. If you keep your mouth shut you will never put your foot in it.
22. In levying taxes and in shearing sheep it is well to stop when you get down to the skin.
23. An Irishman can be worried by the consciousness that there is nothing to worry about.
24. It is a foolish man that hears all he hears.
25. It is a mean thief, or a successful author, that plunders the dead.
26. It is as easy to give advice to yourself as to others, and as useless.
27. The man that leaves no will after his death had little will before his death.
28. Many social visits you think paid to yourself are paid to your bottles.
29. Marriage is a meal where the soup is better than the dessert.

30. The modern king has become a vermiform appendix: useless when quiet; when obtrusive, in danger of removal.
31. Music is another lady that talks charmingly and says nothing.
32. No man can have a reasonable opinion of women until he has long lost interest in hair restorers.
33. Often a convert is zealous not through piety, but because of the novelty of his experience.
34. The perjurer's mother told white lies.
35. The person that always says just what he thinks at last gets just what he deserves.
36. A politician is like quicksilver; if you try to put your finger on him, you will find nothing under it.
37. Practical prayer is harder on the soles of your shoes than on the knees of your trousers.
38. The reason there are so many imbeciles among imprisoned criminals is that an imbecile is so foolish even a detective can detect him.
39. Revenge is often like biting a dog because the dog bit you.
40. Show me a genuine case of platonic friendship, and I shall show you two old or homely faces.
41. The smaller the head, the bigger the dream.
42. Some men are like a clock on a roof; they are useful only to the neighbors.
43. Some men can live up to their loftiest ideals without ever going higher than a basement.
44. The statesman shears the sheep, the politician skins them.
45. There are ten church members by inheritance for one by conviction.
46. There should be more in American liberty than the privilege we enjoy of insulting the President with impunity.
47. Those that think it permissible to tell white lies soon grow color-blind.
48. Those who live in stone houses should not throw glass.
49. The three most important events of human life are equally devoid of reason: birth, marriage, and death.
50. Ugliness is a point of view: an ulcer is wonderful to a pathologist.

51. We smile at the women who are eagerly following the fashions in dress whilst we are as eagerly following the fashions in thought.
52. When there is no will, there is no way for the lawyers.
53. Why is the word 'tongue' feminine in Greek, Latin, Italian, Spanish, French, and German?
54. The worst misfortune that can happen to an ordinary man is to have an extraordinary father.

OSLER, William, 1849–1919
Canadian physician, writer, and teacher of medicine.
1. The desire to take medicine is perhaps the greatest feature which distinguishes man from animals.
2. The natural man has only two primal passions—to get and to beget.
3. There are only two sorts of doctors: those who practice with their brains, and those who practice with their tongues.

OSTENSO, Martha, 1900–1963, *Norwegian-American novelist.*
Edith was a little country bounded on the north, south, east, and west by Edith.

OVERBURY, Sir Thomas, 1581–1613, *English poet.*
The man who has nothing to boast of but his illustrious ancestors is like a potato—the only good belonging to him is under the ground.

OVID, 43 B.C.–A.D. 17?, *Roman poet.*
1. Chaste is she whom no one has asked.
2. If Jupiter hurled his thunderbolt as often as men sinned, he would soon be out of thunderbolts.
3. It is annoying to be honest to no purpose.
4. Let the man who does not wish to be idle fall in love.

PAIN, Barry, 1865–1928, *English humorist and parodist.*
1. Buy visiting cards for the cat; she knows a lot more cats than we know people.

2. Don't answer back if you're out to make money, but do if you're out for enjoyment.

PAINE, Thomas, 1737–1809
American political philosopher, revolutionist, and author.
It would have approached nearer to the idea of miracle if Jonah had swallowed the whale.

PALLADAS, *c.* A.D. 400, *Greek epigrammatist.*
Every woman is a source of annoyance, but she has two good seasons, the one in her bridal chamber and the other in her grave.

PALMERSTON, Lord, 1784–1865, *English statesman.*
1. The best thing for the inside of a man is the outside of a horse.
2. Dirt is not dirt, but only matter in the wrong place.

PARKER, Dorothy, 1893–1967
American wit, poet, and short-story writer.
1. Brevity is the soul of lingerie.
2. A girl's best friend is her mutter.
3. Men seldom make passes at girls who wear glasses.
4. The only 'ism' Hollywood believes in is plagiarism.
5. She ran the whole gamut of the emotions from A to B.

PASCAL, Blaise, 1623–1662
French scientist, mathematician, and philosopher.
1. Had Cleopatra's nose been shorter, the whole face of the world would have been different.
2. I have made this a rather long letter because I haven't had time to make it shorter.
3. If all men knew what each said of the other, there would not be four friends in the world.
4. The last thing we decide in writing a book is what to put first.
5. Those we call the ancients were really new in everything.
6. To be a real philosopher one must be able to laugh at philosophy.

PEACOCK, Thomas Love, 1785–1866
English novelist and poet.

1. I never failed to convince an audience that the best thing they could do was to go away.
2. If 'ifs' and 'ands' were pots and pans, there'd be no work for tinkers.
3. The policeman who was sent down to examine, says my house has been broken open on the most scientific principles.
4. There are two reasons for drinking: one is, when you are thirsty, to cure it; the other, when you are not thirsty, to prevent it.

PEPYS, Samuel, 1633–1703, *English diarist.*

1. A good honest and painful sermon.
2. I find my wife has something in her gizzard that only wants an opportunity of being provoked to bring it up.
3. I went out to see him hanged, drawn, and quartered, which was done, he looking as cheerful as any man could do in that condition.
4. My wife, poor wretch, is troubled with her lonely life.
5. The silk suit cost me much money, and I pray God to make me able to pay for it.
6. Strange to say what delight we married people have to see these poor fools decoyed into our condition.

PHELPS, William Lyon, 1865–1943
American educator and literary critic.

1. At a certain age some people's minds close up; they live on their intellectual fat.
2. A cold is both positive and negative; sometimes the Eyes have it and sometimes the Nose.
3. I divide all readers into two classes: those who read to remember and those who read to forget.
4. If I were running the world I would have it rain only between 2 and 5 a.m.—anyone who was out then ought to get wet.
5. This is the final test of a gentleman: his respect for those who can be of no possible service to him.

6. Nature makes boys and girls lovely to look upon so they can be tolerated until they acquire some sense.

PINERO, Sir Arthur Wing, 1855–1934, *English dramatist.*

1. A financier is a pawnbroker with imagination.
2. How many 'coming men' has one known! Where on earth do they all go to?
3. If there were many more like her, the stock of halos would give out.
4. Married men are viler than bachelors.
5. A married woman's as old as her husband makes her feel.
6. Regret is a woman's natural food—she thrives upon it.
7. She's six and forty; and I wish nothing worse to happen to any woman.

PITT, William, 1759–1806, *English statesman and prime minister.*

1. Don't tell me of a man's being able to talk sense; everyone can talk sense—can he talk nonsense?
2. It was a saying of Lord Chatham that the parks were the lungs of London.
3. Poverty of course is no disgrace, but it is damned annoying.

PLANCHÉ, James Robinson, 1796–1880, *English dramatist.*

1. Better be an old man's darling than become a young man's slave.
2. Nothing is so impudent as Success—unless it be those she favours.

PLATO, 427?–347 B.C.

Greek philosopher, pupil of Socrates, and teacher of Aristotle.

1. The Athenians do not mind a man being clever, as long as he does not impart his cleverness to others.
2. A boy is, of all wild beasts, the most difficult to manage.
3. Man is a two-legged animal without feathers.
4. O ye Gods, grant us what is good whether we pray for it or not, but keep evil from us even though we pray for it.
5. Poets utter great and wise things which they do not themselves understand.

6. Wise men talk because they have something to say; fools, because they have to say something.

PLUTARCH, A.D. 46?–120? *Greek biographer.*

It is indeed desirable to be well descended, but the glory belongs to our ancestors.

POE, Edgar Allan, 1809–1849, *American poet, author, and editor.*

1. The dearth of genius in America is owing to the continual teasing of mosquitoes.
2. I have great faith in fools; self-confidence my friends call it.
3. Of puns it has been said that they who most dislike them are least able to utter them.
4. The people have nothing to do with the laws but to obey them.

POLLOCK, Channing, 1880–1946

American critic, dramatist, novelist, and lecturer.

1. A critic is a legless man who teaches running.
2. He admits that there are two sides to every question—his own and the wrong side.
3. No man in the world has more courage than the man who can stop after eating one peanut.
4. She wore a silk jersey dress that held fast going around curves.

POPE, Alexander, 1688–1744, *English poet.*

1. Amusement is the happiness of those who cannot think.
2. Blessed is he who expects nothing for he shall never be disappointed.
3. A family is but too often a commonwealth of malignants.
4. Histories are more full of examples of the fidelity of dogs than of friends.
5. I am dying, sir, of a hundred good symptoms.
6. Some people will never learn anything, for this reason, because they understand everything too soon.
7. You beat your pate, and fancy wit will come: knock as you please, there's nobody at home.

PRAED, William Mackworth, 1802–1839
English humorous poet.

Forgotten—like a maiden speech, which all men praise, but none remember.

PRENTICE, George D., 1802–1870
American journalist and humorist.

1. About the only person we ever heard of that wasn't spoiled by being lionized was a Jew named Daniel.
2. A bare assertion is not necessarily the naked truth.
3. Be gentle in old age; peevishness is worse in second childhood than in first.
4. It is our will to speak the plain truth and, what is better, our wont.
5. Many a man keeps on drinking till he hasn't a coat to either his back or his stomach.
6. One of the very best of all earthly possessions is self-possession.
7. A pin has as much head as some authors, and a good deal more point.
8. Some members of Congress would best promote the country's peace by holding their own.
9. Some old women and men grow bitter with age; the more their teeth drop out, the more biting they get.
10. Some people use one half their ingenuity to get into debt, and the other half to avoid paying it.
11. What man wants: all he can get; what woman wants: all she can't get.
12. When a young man complains that a young lady has no heart, it is a pretty certain sign that she has his.

PRIESTLEY, John Boynton, born 1894
English novelist, dramatist, and critic.

A loving wife will do anything for her husband except stop criticizing and trying to improve him.

QUARLES, Francis, 1592–1644, *English poet.*

1. Friendship will not continue to the end which is begun for an end.

2. The goods we spend we keep; and what we save we lose; and only what we lose we have.
3. Physicians of all men are most happy; what good success they have, the world proclaimeth, and what faults they commit, the earth covereth.

RABELAIS, François, 1495?–1553, *French humorist and satirist.*

1. God forbid that I should be out of debt, as if, indeed, I could not be trusted.
2. He was subject to a kind of disease, which at that time they called lack of money.
3. I never sleep comfortably except when I am at a sermon.
4. I owe much; I have nothing; the rest I leave to the poor.
5. Keep running after a dog, and he will never bite you.
6. If you wish to avoid seeing a fool you must first break your mirror.
7. Not that I mistrust her virtue, but—she is a woman. There lies the suspicion.
8. When I drink, I think; and when I think, I drink.

RASPE, Rudolph Erich, 1737–1794
German mineralogist and creator of 'Baron Munchausen'.

If anyone doubts my veracity, I can only say that I pity his lack of faith.

RAY, John, 1627–1705, *English chronicler.*

1. Children suck the mother when they are young, and the father when they are grown.
2. I love thee like pudding; if thou wert pie, I'd eat thee.
3. Wedlock is a padlock.
4. What she wants in up and down she hath in round about.

READE, Charles, 1814–1884, *English novelist and dramatist.*

We go on fancying that each man is thinking of us, but he is not; he is like us: he is thinking of himself.

RENAN, Joseph Ernest, 1823–1890
French philologist, philosopher, and historian.

1. The ignorance of French society gives one a rough sense o the infinite.
2. O Lord, if there is a Lord, save my soul, if I have a soul.

RENARD, Jules, 1864–1910, *French novelist and dramatist.*
A cold in the head causes less suffering then an idea.

RENIER, Dr. G. J., 1892–1962, *Anglo-Dutch historian and authc*

1. The English never like to go further than their owr experience.
2. The world is inhabited by two species of human beings mankind and the English.

RICHELIEU, Duke of, 1585–1642
French cardinal and statesman.

If you give me six lines written by the most honest man I will find something in them to hang him.

RICHTER, Jean Paul, 1847–1937
English art critic and historian.

1. Spring makes everything young again except man.
2. A variety of nothing is better than a monotony of something.

RIVAROL, Comte de, 1753–1801, *French critic and satirist.*

1. Friendship among women is only a suspension of hostilities
2. It is, no doubt, an immense advantage to have done nothing but one should not abuse it.
3. The personal pronoun 'I' should be the coat of arms o some individuals.

ROCHE, James Jeffrey, 1847–1908
American journalist, poet, and author.

1. Be not concerned if thou findest thyself in possession o unexpected wealth; Allah will provide an unexpectec use for it.

2. Pay as you go, but not if you intend going for good.
3. Some men borrow books; some men steal books; and others beg presentation copies from the author.
4. To be constant in love to one is good; to be constant to many is great.

ROCHESTER, John Wilmot, Earl of, 1647–1680, *English poet.*

1. Before I got married I had six theories about bringing up children; now I have six children, and no theories.
2. Womankind more joy discovers Making fools than taking lovers.

ROGERS, Samuel, 1763–1855, *English poet.*

1. Her tea she sweetens, as she sips, with scandal.
2. It does not much signify whom one marries, as one is sure to find next morning that it is someone else.

ROGERS, Will, 1879–1935
American humorist, motion-picture actor, and lecturer.

1. All I know is what I read in the papers.
2. America is a nation that conceives many odd inventions for getting somewhere but can think of nothing to do when it gets there.
3. Congressional investigations are for the benefit of photographers.
4. Everybody is ignorant, only on different subjects.
5. Everything is funny, as long as it is happening to somebody else.
6. Gentlemen, you have just been listening to that Chinese sage, On Too Long.
7. The good old horse-and-buggy days: then you lived until you died and not until you were just run over.
8. A holding company is a thing where you hand an accomplice the goods while the policeman searches you.
9. I don't make jokes; I just watch the government and report the facts.
10. I never expected to see the day when girls would get sunburned in the places they now do.

11. I never lack material for my humor column when Congress is in session.
12. In Hollywood the woods are full of people that learned to write but evidently can't read.
13. The income tax has made more liars out of the American people than gold has.
14. Maybe *ain't* ain't so correct, but I notice that lots of folks who ain't using *ain't*, ain't eating.
15. My folks didn't come over on the *Mayflower*, but they were there to meet the boat.
16. The nation is prosperous on the whole, but how much prosperity is there in a hole?
17. No party is as bad as its leaders.
18. One third of the people in the United States promote while the other two thirds provide.
19. The only time people dislike gossip is when you gossip about them.
20. Our country has plenty of good five-cent cigars, but the trouble is they charge fifteen cents for them.
21. Our foreign dealings are an open book—generally a check-book.
22. The Republicans have their splits right after election, and Democrats have theirs just before an election.
23. So live that you wouldn't be ashamed to sell the family parrot to the town gossip.
24. Spinning a rope's a lot of fun—providing your neck ain't in it.
25. There is no more independence in politics than there is in jail.
26. Ukulele: a so-called musical instrument which, when listened to, you cannot tell whether one is playing on it or just monkeying with it.
27. The United States never lost a war or won a conference.
28. What the country needs is dirtier fingernails and cleaner minds.
29. With Congress, every time they make a joke it's a law; and every time they make a law it's a joke.
30. Wrigley was the first man to discover that American jaws must wag; so why not give them something to wag against?

ROMBERG, Sigmund, 1887–1951, *American composer.*
A love song is just a caress set to music.

ROOSEVELT, Franklin Delano, 1882–1945
President of the United States.
1. The ablest man I ever met is the man you think you are.
2. A conservative is a man with two perfectly good legs who has never learned to walk.
3. It got to a point where I had to get a haircut or a violin.
4. A radical is a man with both feet firmly planted in the air.
5. A reactionary is a somnambulist walking backward.
6. When you get to the end of your rope, tie a knot and hang on.

ROOSEVELT, Theodore, 1858–1919
President of the United States.
1. I am only an average man but, by George, I work harder at it than the average man.
2. I suppose I overdo it, but when I'm mad at a man I want to climb right up his chest.
3. I think there is only one quality worse than hardness of heart and that is softness of head.
4. I took the Canal Zone and let Congress debate, and while the debate goes on the canal does too.
5. A man who has never gone to school may steal from a freight car; but if he has a university education, he may steal the whole railroad.
6. The most successful politician is he who says what everybody is thinking most often and in the loudest voice.

ROSSINI, Gioacchino Antonio, 1792–1868
Italian operatic composer.
1. Give me a laundry list and I'll set it to music.
2. How wonderful opera would be if there were no singers.
3. Wagner has beautiful moments but awful quarter hours.

ROSTAND, Edmond, 1868–1918, *French poet and playwright.*
To offend is my pleasure; I love to be hated.

6

ROSTAND, Jean, born 1894, *French littérateur.*

My sincerity goes to the point of suspecting the sincerity of the pessimists.

ROUSSEAU, Jean Jacques, 1712–1778
French philosopher and author.

1. Happiness: a good bank account, a good cook, and a good digestion.
2. Take away from our learned men the pleasure of making themselves heard, learning would then be nothing to them.
3. There is a period of life when we go backwards as we advance.
4. To write a love letter we must begin without knowing what we intend to say, and end without knowing what we have written.

ROUX, Joseph, 1834–1886, *French priest and epigrammatist.*

God often visits us, but most of the time we are not at home.

ROWLAND, Helen, 1875–1950
American humorous columnist and author.

1. A bachelor gets tangled up with a lot of women in order to avoid getting tied up to one.
2. A bachelor never quite gets over the idea that he is a thing of beauty and a boy forever.
3. A Bachelor of Arts is one who makes love to a lot of women, and yet has the art to remain a bachelor.
4. Before marriage, a man will lie awake all night thinking about something you said; after marriage, he'll fall asleep before you finish saying it.
5. Every man wants a woman to appeal to his better side, his nobler instincts and his higher nature—and another woman to help him forget them.
6. The follies which a man regrets most in his life are those which he didn't commit when he had the opportunity.
7. A fool and her money are soon courted.

8. From the day on which she weighs 140, the chief excitement of a woman's life consists in spotting women who are fatter than she is.
9. A good woman is known by what she does; a good man by what he doesn't.
10. Grass widow: the angel a man loved, the human being he married, and the devil he divorced.
11. Half a love is better than none.
12. The hardest task of a girl's life is to prove to a man that his intentions are serious.
13. The honeymoon is not over until we cease to stifle our sighs and begin to stifle our yawns.
14. A husband is what is left of the lover after the nerve has been extracted.
15. In olden times sacrifices were made at the altar—a custom which is still continued.
16. In the spring a young man's fancy lightly turns—and turns—and turns.
17. It's as hard to get a man to stay home after you've married him as it was to get him to go home before you married him.
18. It is easier to keep half a dozen lovers guessing than to keep one lover after he has stopped guessing.
19. It isn't tying himself to one woman that a man dreads when he thinks of marrying; it's separating himself from all the others.
20. It takes one woman twenty years to make a man of her son, and another woman twenty minutes to make a fool of him.
21. Love is woman's eternal spring and man's eternal fall.
22. Love, the quest; marriage, the conquest; divorce, the inquest.
23. A man loses his illusions first, his teeth second, and his follies last.
24. A man marries one woman to escape from many others, and then chases many others to forget he's married to one.
25. A man never knows how to say good-bye; a woman never knows when to say it.
26. A man's ideal woman is the one he passes with a worshipful bow—when he's on his way to call on the other woman.

27. A man snatches the first kiss, pleads for the second, demands the third, takes the fourth, accepts the fifth—and endures all the rest.
28. A man will joyfully pay a lawyer five hundred dollars for untying the knot that he begrudged a clergyman fifty dollars for tying.
29. Marriage: a souvenir of love.
30. Marriage is the miracle that transforms a kiss from a pleasure into a duty, and a life from a luxury into a necessity.
31. Matrimony is a bargain, and somebody has to get the worst of the bargain.
32. Never trust a husband too far, nor a bachelor too near.
33. No man can understand why a woman should prefer a good reputation to a good time.
34. Nobody is as sophisticated as a boy of nineteen who is just recovering from a baby-grand passion.
35. Nowadays most women grow old gracefully; most men, disgracefully.
36. One man's folly is another man's wife.
37. The only original thing about some men is original sin.
38. Soft, sweet things with a lot of fancy dressing—that's what a little boy loves to eat and a grown man prefers to marry.
39. The softer a man's head, the louder his socks.
40. Some men feel that the only thing they owe the woman who marries them is a grudge.
41. Some men think that being married to a woman means merely seeing her in the mornings instead of in the evenings.
42. Some widowers are bereaved; others, relieved.
43. Telling lies is a fault in a boy, an art in a lover, an accomplishment in a bachelor, and second nature in a married woman.
44. There are more ways of killing a man's love than by strangling it to death, but that's the usual way.
45. To a woman the first kiss is just the end of the beginning; to a man it is the beginning of the end.
46. Wedding: the point at which a man stops toasting a woman and begins roasting her.

47. When a girl marries she exchanges the attentions of many men for the inattention of one.
48. When a man makes a woman his wife, it's the highest compliment he can pay her, and it's usually the last.
49. When it comes to making love, a girl can always listen so much faster than a man can talk.
50. When mother-in-law comes in at the door, love flies out at the window.
51. When you see a married couple coming down the street, the one who is two or three steps ahead is the one that's mad.
52. When you see what some girls marry, you realize how they must hate to work for a living.
53. A woman marries the first time for love, the second time for companionship, the third time for support, and the rest of the time just from habit.
54. Woman: the peg on which the wit hangs his jest, the preacher his text, the cynic his grouch, and the sinner his justification.
55. A woman's last resort is henna; a man's, Gehenna.

RUNYON, Damon, 1884–1946
American journalist and short-story writer.

1. Much as he is opposed to lawbreaking, he is not bigoted about it.
2. The race is not always to the swift, nor the battle to the strong—but that's the way to bet.

RUSKIN, John, 1819–1900, *English art critic and social reformer.*

1. An artist should be fit for the best society and keep out of it.
2. The first of all English games is making money.
3. Going by railroad I do not consider as travelling . . . it is merely being 'sent' to a place, and very little different from being a parcel.
4. He thinks by infection, catching an opinion like a cold.
5. There is hardly anything in the world that some man cannot make a little worse and sell a little cheaper.
6. When a man is wrapped up in himself he makes a pretty small package.

7. Writers like the present critic . . . deserve more respect; the respect due to honest, hopeless, helpless imbecility.
8. You knock a man into the ditch, and then you tell him to remain content in the position in which Providence has placed him.

RUSSELL, Bertrand, 1872–1970
English philosopher, mathematician, and author.

1. Christian humility is preached by the clergy, but practised only by the lower classes.
2. Even in civilized mankind faint traces of a monogamic instinct can sometimes be perceived.
3. Even when the experts all agree, they may well be mistaken.
4. Few people can be happy unless they hate some other person, nation, or creed.
5. The fundamental defect of fathers is that they want their children to be a credit to them.
6. In America law and custom alike are based upon the dreams of spinsters.
7. Most people would die sooner than think; in fact, they do so.
8. The people who are regarded as moral luminaries are those who forgo ordinary pleasures themselves and find compensation in interfering with the pleasures of others.
9. The trouble with the world is that the stupid are cocksure and the intelligent full of doubt.
10. We have two kinds of morality side by side: one which we preach but do not practise, and another which we practise but seldom preach.

SADLEIR, Michael, 1888–1957, *English author and publisher.*
The earliest bird gets the most worms.

SAINTE-BEUVE, Charles Augustin, 1804–1869
French critic and poet.
A critic is a man whose watch is five minutes ahead of other people's watches.

SAINT-GAUDENS, Augustus, 1848–1907, *American sculptor.*
What garlic is to salad, insanity is to art.

'SAKI', 1870–1916

Pen-name of Hector Hugh Munro, English short-story writer and novelist.

1. Because he didn't ask for titles and honours and dignities, but only for immense wealth, these other things came to him also.
2. Bernard Shaw had discovered himself and gave ungrudgingly of his discovery to the world.
3. The cook was a good cook, as cooks go; and as cooks go, she went.
4. Her frocks come from Paris, but she wears them with a strong English accent.
5. He's simply got the instinct for being unhappy highly developed.
6. I'm living so far beyond my income that we may almost be said to be living apart.
7. No more privacy than a goldfish.
8. She's so fond of talking of certain pictures as 'growing on one' as though they were a sort of fungus.
9. There's nothing in Christianity or Buddhism that quite matches the sympathetic unselfishness of an oyster.
10. Waldo is one of those people who would be enormously improved by death.
11. The Western custom of one wife and hardly any mistresses.
12. Women and elephants never forget an injury.

SALTUS, Edgar, 1855–1921, *American author.*

1. Divorce is like matrimony: a fellow has got to go through it three or four times before he knows how.
2. It is better to have loved your wife than never to have loved at all.
3. Society would be delightful were all women married and all men single.

SANDBURG, Carl, 1878–1967, *American poet and biographer.*

1. I won't take my religion from any man who never works except with his mouth.
2. Slang is language that takes off its coat, spits on its hands, and goes to work.

SANTAYANA, George, 1863–1952
American poet, philosopher, and essayist.

1. An artist may visit a museum, but only a pedant can live there.
2. Broad-mindedness is the result of flattening high-mindedness out.
3. Declarations of Independence make nobody really independent.
4. The Difficult is that which can be done immediately; the Impossible that which takes a little longer.
5. Fanaticism consists in redoubling your effort when you have forgotten your aim.
6. It is a great advantage for a system of philosophy to be substantially true.
7. Life is not a spectacle or a feast; it is a predicament.
8. There is no cure for birth or death save to enjoy the interval.
9. Those who cannot remember the past are condemned to repeat it.

SARGENT, John Singer, 1856–1925, *American portrait painter.*

Every time I paint a portrait I lose a friend.

SCHLEGEL, August Wilhelm von, 1767–1845
German editor, translator, and man of letters.

The historian is a prophet looking backwards.

SCHOPENHAUER, Arthur, 1788–1860, *German philosopher.*

1. The first forty years of life give us the text; the next thirty supply the commentary.
2. It is difficult to keep quiet if you have nothing to do.
3. Reading is thinking with someone else's head instead of one's own.

SCHUMANN, Robert, 1810–1856, *German composer.*

In order to compose, all you need to do is remember a tune that nobody else has thought of.

SCOTT, Sir Walter, 1771–1832

Scotch novelist, poet, historian, and biographer.

1. Her face was of that doubtful kind That wins the heart but not the mind.
2. It requires no small talents to be a decided bore.
3. Like all rogues, he was a great calumniator of the fair sex.
4. Many of our cares are but a morbid way of looking at our privileges.
5. The most effectual way of conferring a favour is condescending to accept one.
6. Please return this book; I find that though many of my friends are poor arithmeticians, they are nearly all good bookkeepers.
7. When a man hasn't a good reason for doing a thing, he has a good reason for letting it alone.

SELDEN, John, 1584–1654

English jurist, scholar, and statesman.

Preachers say, do as I say, not as I do.

SENECA, Lucius Annaeus, *c.* 5 B.C.–A.D. 65

Roman stoic philosopher and dramatist.

It is an extreme evil to depart from the company of the living before you die.

SÉVIGNÉ, Marquise de, 1626–1696

French lady of fashion and letter writer.

1. Fortune is always on the side of the biggest battalions.
2. He lacked only a few vices to be perfect.
3. The more I see of men the more I admire dogs.
4. Religious people spend so much time with their confessors because they like to talk about themselves.

SHAKESPEARE, William, 1564–1616

English poet and dramatist.

1. A barber's chair fits all buttocks.
2. Better a witty fool than a foolish wit.
3. Britain is a world by itself, and we will nothing pay for wearing our own noses.

4. Civil as an orange, and something of that jealous complexion.
5. Commit the oldest sins the newest kind of ways.
6. Doubt not her care should be to comb your noddle with a three-legged stool.
7. Everyone can master a grief but he that has it.
8. The first thing we do, let's kill all the lawyers.
9. Give every man thy ear but few thy voice.
10. God has given you one face, and you make yourself another.
11. God made him, and therefore let him pass for a man.
12. Gratiano speaks an infinite deal of nothing, more than any man in all Venice.
13. He draweth out the thread of his verbosity finer than the staple of his argument.
14. He is winding the watch of his wit; by and by it will strike.
15. He that dies this year is quit for the next.
16. How ill grey hairs become a fool and jester.
17. I am not only witty in myself, but the cause that wit is in other men.
18. I am Sir Oracle, and when I ope my lips let no dog bark.
19. I can easier teach twenty what were good to be done than be one of the twenty to follow mine own teaching.
20. I do desire we may be better strangers.
21. I had rather have a fool to make me merry than experience to make me sad.
22. I have no other but a woman's reason; I think him so because I think him so.
23. I prythee, take the cork out of my mouth that I may drink thy tidings.
24. I thank God I am as honest as any man living that is an old man and no honester than I.
25. I will praise any man that will praise me.
26. In converting Jews to Christians, you raise the price of pork.
27. Maids want nothing but husbands, and when they have them, they want everything.
28. Many a good hanging prevents a bad marriage.
29. A miser grows rich by seeming poor; an extravagant man grows poor by seeming rich.

30. O, he is as tedious as a tired horse, a railing wife; worse than a smoky house.
31. O that he were here to write me down an ass.
32. 'So-so' is good, very good, very excellent maxim; and yet it is not; it is but so-so.
33. Stabbed with a white wench's black eye: shot through the ear with a love-song.
34. The tartness of his face sours ripe grapes.
35. A terrible oath, with a swaggering accent sharply twanged off, gives manhood more approbation than ever proof itself would have earned him.
36. That thou art my son, I have partly thy mother's word, partly my own opinion.
37. There's not a note of mine that's worth the noting.
38. There was never yet philosopher that could endure the toothache patiently.
39. To be slow in words is a woman's only virtue.
40. Two women placed together make cold weather.
41. Unbidden guests are often welcomest when they are gone.
42. Vanity keeps persons in favour with themselves who are out of favour with all others.
43. Were kisses all the joy in bed, one woman would another wed.
44. When I said I would die a bachelor, I did not think I would live till I were married.
45. When I tell him he hates flatterers, he says he does, being then the most flattered.
46. When my love swears that she is made of truth, I do believe her though I know she lies.
47. Who wears his wit in his belly and his guts in his head.
48. A withered hermit, five-score winters worn, Might shake off fifty, looking in her eye.
49. You are one of those that will not serve God if the devil bid you.
50. You rise to play and go to bed to work.
51. You shall never take her without her answer, unless you take her without her tongue.
52. A young man married is a man that's marred.

SHAW, George Bernard, 1856–1950

Anglo-Irish dramatist, critic, novelist, social reformer, and wit.

1. All my life, affection has been showered upon me, and every forward step I have made has been taken in spite of it.
2. Assassination is the extreme form of censorship.
3. An asylum for the sane would be empty in America.
4. Baseball has the great advantage over cricket of being sooner ended.
5. Beauty is all very well at sight, but who can look at it when it has been in the house three days?
6. The best reformers the world has ever seen are those who commence on themselves.
7. The British churchgoer prefers a severe preacher because he thinks a few home truths will do his neighbours no harm.
8. Cannons are not trade; they are enterprise.
9. Censorship ends in logical completeness when nobody is allowed to read any books except the books nobody can read.
10. The chief objection to playing wind instruments is that it prolongs the life of the player.
11. The churches must learn humility as well as teach it.
12. Common people do not pray; they only beg.
13. Decency is indecency's conspiracy of silence.
14. Democracy substitutes election by the incompetent many for appointment by the corrupt few.
15. The devil can quote Shakespeare for his own purpose.
16. Do not do unto others as you would they should do unto you; their tastes may not be the same.
17. England and America are two countries separated by the same language.
18. An Englishman does everything on principle: he fights you on patriotic principles; he robs you on business principles; he enslaves you on imperial principles.
19. An Englishman thinks he is moral when he is only uncomfortable.
20. Englishmen never will be slaves; they are free to do whatever the Government and public opinion allow them to do.

21. Every man over forty is a scoundrel.
22. Everything happens to everybody sooner or later if there is time enough.
23. Except during the nine months before he draws his first breath, no man manages his affairs as well as a tree does.
24. Few people think more than two or three times a year; I have made an international reputation for myself by thinking once or twice a week.
25. The fickleness of the women I love is only equalled by the infernal constancy of the women who love me.
26. First love is only a little foolishness and a lot of curiosity.
27. The formation of a young lady's mind and character usually consists in telling her lies.
28. Gambling promises the poor what property performs for the rich—something for nothing.
29. A gentleman is a gentleman the world over; loafers differ.
30. The golden rule is that there are no golden rules.
31. The great advantage of a hotel is that it's a refuge from home life.
32. Greek scholars are privileged men; few of them know Greek, and most of them know nothing else.
33. Hamlet's experiences simply could not have happened to a plumber.
34. He's a devout believer in the department of witchcraft called medical science.
35. He's a man of great common sense and good taste—meaning thereby a man without originality or moral courage.
36. He who can, does; he who cannot, teaches.
37. He who would reform himself must first reform society.
38. Human beings are the only animals of which I am thoroughly and cravenly afraid.
39. The ideal love affair is one conducted by post.
40. I'm only a beer teetotaller, not a champagne teetotaller; I don't like beer.
41. I dislike feeling at home when I'm abroad.
42. I enjoy convalescence; it is the part that makes the illness worth while.
43. I have never thought much of the courage of a lion-tamer; inside the cage he is, at least, safe from other men.

44. I often quote myself; it adds spice to my conversation.
45. I strive automatically to bring the world into harmony with my own nature.
46. If a great man could make us understand him we should hang him.
47. If all economists were laid end to end, they would not reach a conclusion.
48. If ever I utter an oath again may my soul be blasted to eternal damnation.
49. If history repeats itself, and the unexpected always happens, how incapable must man be of learning from experience!
50. If you are a bore, strive to be a rascal also so that you may not discredit virtue.
51. Imprisonment, as it exists today, is a worse crime than any of those committed by its victims.
52. In heaven an angel is nobody in particular.
53. In literature the ambition of the novice is to acquire the literary language; the struggle of the adept is to get rid of it.
54. It is a woman's business to get married as soon as possible, and a man's to keep unmarried as long as he can.
55. Kings are not born; they are made by universal hallucination.
56. Lack of money is the root of all evil.
57. Ladies and gentlemen are permitted to have friends in the kennel but not in the kitchen.
58. A learned man is an idler who kills time by study.
59. Leave it to the coward to make a religion of his cowardice by preaching humility.
60. The liar's punishment is not in the least that he is not believed, but that he cannot believe anyone else.
61. A lifetime of happiness! No man alive could bear it; it would be hell on earth.
62. Love is a gross exaggeration of the difference between one person and everybody else.
63. A man never tells you anything until you contradict him.
64. A man without an address is a vagabond; a man with two addresses is a libertine.

65. Marriage is all very well, but it isn't romance; there's nothing wrong in it.
66. Marriage is popular because it combines the maximum of temptation with the maximum of opportunity.
67. A married man can do anything he likes if his wife doesn't mind; a widower can't be too careful.
68. Martyrdom is the only way in which a man can become famous without ability.
69. Men have to do some awfully mean things to keep up their respectability.
70. Men like conventions because men made them.
71. A miracle is an event which creates faith; that is the purpose and nature of miracles.
72. The mistake was in not forbidding the serpent; then Adam would have eaten the serpent.
73. The more things a man is ashamed of, the more respectable he is.
74. The most anxious man in a prison is the warden.
75. My specialty is being right when other people are wrong.
76. My way of joking is to tell the truth; it's the funniest joke in the world.
77. No sooner had Jesus knocked over the dragon of superstition than Paul boldly set it on its legs again in the name of Jesus.
78. Nothing soothes me more after a long and maddening course of pianoforte recitals than to sit and have my teeth drilled.
79. Obscenity can be found in every book except the telephone directory.
80. The 100 per cent American is 99 per cent an idiot.
81. The only way a woman can provide for herself decently is to be good to some man that can afford to be good to her.
82. The other evening, feeling rather in want of a headache, I bethought me that I had not been to a music hall for a long time.
83. Patriotism is your conviction that this country is superior to all other countries because you were born in it.
84. A perpetual holiday is a good working definition of hell.

85. A pessimist thinks everybody as nasty as himself, and hates them for it.
86. Put an Irishman on the spit, and you can always get another Irishman to turn him.
87. Reading made Don Quixote a gentleman, but believing what he read made him mad.
88. Rich men without convictions are more dangerous in modern society than poor women without chastity.
89. Science is always wrong: it never solves a problem without creating ten more.
90. The secret of being miserable is to have leisure to bother about whether you are happy or not.
91. Self-denial is not a virtue; it is only the effect of prudence on rascality.
92. Success covers a multitude of blunders.
93. Take care to get what you like, or you will end by liking what you get.
94. The test of a man or woman's breeding is how they behave in a quarrel.
95. There are fools everywhere, even in asylums.
96. There are no secrets better kept than the secrets that everybody guesses.
97. There are not competent people enough in the world to go round; somebody must get the incompetent lawyers and doctors.
98. There are only two classes in good society in England: the equestrian classes and the neurotic classes.
99. There is no love sincerer than the love of food.
100. There is no satisfaction in hanging a man who does not object to it.
101. There is not much harm in a lion; he has no ideals, no religion, no politics, no chivalry, no gentility.
102. There is only one religion, though there are a hundred versions of it.
103. There may be some doubt as to who are the best people to have charge of children, but there can be no doubt that parents are the worst.
104. The things most people want to know about are usually none of their business.

105. The truth is the one thing that nobody will believe.
106. Virtue is insufficient temptation.
107. We are told that when Jehovah created the world he saw that it was good; what would he say now?
108. What God hath joined together no man shall ever put asunder; God will take care of that.
109. What is the matter with the poor is poverty; what is the matter with the rich is uselessness.
110. What man is capable of the insane self-conceit of believing that an eternity of himself would be tolerable even to himself?
111. What really flatters a man is that you think him worth flattering.
112. When a man wants to murder a tiger he calls it sport; when a tiger wants to murder him, he calls it ferocity.
113. When a stupid man is doing something he is ashamed of, he always declares that it is his duty.
114. When we want to read of the deeds that are done for love, whither do we turn? To the murder column.
115. When you read a biography remember that the truth is never fit for publication.
116. Why was I born with such contemporaries?
117. With the exception of capitalism, there is nothing so revolting as revolution.
118. The worst cliques are those which consist of one man.
119. The writer who aims at producing the platitudes which are 'not for an age but for all time' has his reward in being unreadable in all ages.
120. You don't expect me to know what to say about a play when I don't know who the author is, do you?
121. You must not suppose, because I am a man of letters, that I never tried to earn an honest living.
122. You'll never have a quiet world till you knock the patriotism out of the human race.
123. Youth is a wonderful thing; what a crime to waste it on children.

SHELLEY, Percy Bysshe, 1792–1822, *English poet.*

1. Hell is a city much like London.

2. It is a nose once seen never to be forgotten, and which requires the utmost strength of Christian charity to forgive.

SHENSTONE, William, 1714–1763, *English poet.*

1. Necessity may be the mother of lucrative invention, but it is the death of poetical.
2. A picturesque countenance, rather than one that is esteemed of regular features.

SHERIDAN, Philip Henry, 1831–1888, *American general.*

If I owned Texas and Hell, I'd rent out Texas and live in Hell.

SHERIDAN, Richard Brinsley, 1751–1816, *Irish dramatist.*

1. A damned disinheriting countenance.
2. A fluent tongue is the only thing a mother doesn't like her daughter to resemble her in.
3. From the silence which prevails I conclude Lauderdale has been making a joke.
4. If I reprehend anything in this world, it is the use of my oracular tongue, and a nice derangement of epitaphs!
5. If it is abuse, why one is always sure to hear of it from one damned good-natured friend or another.
6. I think the interpreter is the hardest to be understood of the two.
7. Our ancestors are very good kind of folks, but they are the last people I should choose to have a visiting acquaintance with.
8. The right honourable gentleman is indebted to his memory for his jests, and to his imagination for his facts.
9. She looks like a mended statue, in which the connoisseur may see at once that the head is modern though the trunk's antique.
10. 'Tis safest in matrimony to begin with a little aversion.
11. The quarrel is a very pretty quarrel as it stands; we should only spoil by trying to explain it.

SHERMAN, William Tecumseh, 1820–1891
American general.

1. Grant stood by me when I was crazy, and I stood by him when he was drunk, and now we stand by each other.
2. If forced to choose between the penitentiary and the White House for four years, I would say the penitentiary, thank you.
3. Vox populi, vox humbug.

SHIRLEY, James, 1596–1666, *English dramatic poet.*
A woman and a wet eel both have slippery tails.

SHORTHOUSE, Joseph Henry, 1834–1903, *English novelist.*
Wordsworth's standard of intoxication was miserably low.

SIBELIUS, Jean, 1865–1957, *Finnish composer.*
Pay no attention to what the critics say; there has never been set up a statue in honour of a critic.

SIENKIEWICZ, Henryk, 1846–1916
Polish novelist and short-story writer.
The greater the philosopher, the harder it is for him to answer the questions of the average man.

SIMONDS, Frank H., 1878–1936
American journalist and war correspondent.
There is but one way for a newspaperman to look at a politician, and that is down.

SINCLAIR, Upton, 1878–1968
American novelist and social reformer.
It is difficult to get a man to understand something when his salary depends upon his not understanding it.

SITWELL, Sir Osbert, 1892–1969, *English poet and novelist.*
I am most fond of talking and thinking; that is to say, talking first and thinking afterward.

SKINNER, Cornelia Otis, born 1901
American actress and author.

1. Mosquitoes were using my ankles for filling stations.
2. One learns in life to keep silent and draw one's own confusions.
3. She was permanently waved both as to hair and figure.

SMILES, Samuel, 1812–1904
English author and social reformer.

The shortest way to do many things is to do only one thing at once.

SMITH, Adam, 1723–1790, *Scottish political economist.*

Man is an animal that makes bargains; no other animal does this—no dog exchanges bones with another.

SMITH, Horace, 1779–1849, *English parodist.*

1. Good advice is one of those injuries which a good man ought, if possible, to forgive, but at all events to forget at once.
2. Inconsistency is the only thing in which men are consistent.

SMITH, Logan Pearsall, 1865–1946
English essayist and critic.

1. All my life, as down an abyss without a bottom, I have been pouring vanloads of information into that vacancy of oblivion I call my mind.
2. All reformers, however strict their conscience, live in houses just as big as they can pay for.
3. The denunciation of the young is a necessary part of the hygiene of older people, and greatly assists the circulation of their blood.
4. Don't laugh at a youth for his affectations; he is only trying on one face after another to find his own.
5. Hearts that are delicate and kind, and tongues that are neither—these make the finest company in the world.
6. How I should like to distil my disesteem of my contemporaries into prose so perfect that all of them would have to read it!

7. I hate having new books forced upon me, but how I love cram-throating other people with them.
8. I have been a success: for sixty years I have eaten, and have avoided being eaten.
9. I might give my life for my friend, but he had better not ask me to do up a parcel.
10. If you want to be thought a liar always tell the truth.
11. An improper mind is a perpetual feast.
12. Isn't it odd that flowers are the reproductive organs of the plants they grow on?
13. It is just as well to be a little giddy-pated, if you are to feel at home on this turning earth.
14. It is the wretchedness of being rich that you have to live with rich people.
15. Most people sell their souls and live with a good conscience on the proceeds.
16. One can be bored until boredom becomes a mystical experience.
17. Thank heavens! The sun has gone in, and I don't have to go out and enjoy it.
18. There are few sorrows, however poignant, in which a good income is of no avail.
19. Those who set out to serve both God and Mammon soon discover that there is no God.
20. We are told by moralists with the plainest faces that immorality will spoil our looks.
21. What music is more enchanting than the voices of young people when you can't hear what they say?
22. When they come downstairs from their ivory towers, idealists are apt to walk straight into the gutter.

SMITH, Sydney, 1771–1845

English clergyman, essayist, and wit.

1. As the French say, there are three sexes—men, women, and clergymen.
2. Benevolence is a natural instinct of the human mind; when A sees B in distress, his conscience always urges him to entreat C to help him.

3. The best way of answering a bad argument is to let it go on.
4. Correspondences are like small-clothes before the invention of suspenders; it is impossible to keep them up.
5. Daniel Webster struck me much like a steam engine in trousers.
6. The first receipt to farm well is to be rich.
7. The further he went west, the more convinced he felt that the wise men came from the east.
8. He deserves to be preached to death by wild curates.
9. He has no command over his understanding; it is always getting between his legs and tripping him up.
10. He has not body enough to cover his mind decently; his intellect is improperly exposed.
11. He has occasional flashes of silence that make his conversation perfectly delightful.
12. He has returned from Italy a greater bore than ever; he bores on architecture, painting, statuary, and music.
13. He has spent all his life in letting down buckets into empty wells; and he is frittering away his age in trying to draw them up again.
14. He is remarkably well, considering that he has been remarkably well for so many years.
15. How can a bishop marry? How can he flirt? The most he can say is: 'I will see you in the vestry after service'.
16. I am convinced digestion is the great secret of life.
17. I am just going to pray for you at St. Paul's, but with no very lively hope of success.
18. I hate a woman who seems to be hermetically sealed in the lower regions.
19. I have been looking for a person who disliked gray all my life; let us swear eternal friendship.
20. I have gout, asthma, and seven other maladies, but am otherwise very well.
21. I have no relish for the country; it is a kind of healthy grave.
22. I have the most perfect confidence in your indiscretion.
23. I heard him speak disrespectfully of the equator.
24. I like him and his wife; he is so ladylike, and she's such a perfect gentleman.

25. I must believe in the Apostolic Succession, there being no other way of accounting for the descent of the Bishop of Exeter from Judas Iscariot.
26. I never read a book before reviewing it; it prejudices one so.
27. I think breakfast so pleasant because no one is conceited before one o'clock.
28. If I were to begin life again, I would devote it to music. It is the only cheap and unpunished rapture on earth.
29. In composing, as a general rule, run your pen through every other word you have written; you have no idea what vigour it will give your style.
30. I was so hot here that I found there was nothing left for it but to take off my flesh and sit in my bones.
31. It would be an entertaining change in human affairs to determine everything by minorities; they are almost always in the right.
32. Marriage resembles a pair of shears, so joined that they cannot be separated; often moving in opposite directions, yet always punishing anyone who comes between them.
33. The most solemn and terrible duty of a bishop is the entertainment of the clergy.
34. My handwriting looks as if a swarm of ants, escaping from an ink bottle, had walked over a sheet of paper without wiping their legs.
35. My idea of heaven is eating *pâtés de foie gras* to the sound of trumpets.
36. No furniture is so charming as books, even if you never open them or read a single word.
37. No man should write on Christianity unless he is prepared to go the whole *lamb*.
38. The observances of the church concerning feasts and fasts are tolerably well kept since the rich keep the feasts and the poor the fasts.
39. Poverty is no disgrace to a man, but it is confoundedly inconvenient.
40. The preterpluperfect tense has always occasioned him much uneasiness though he has appeared to the world cheerful and serene.

41. A sparrow fluttering about the church is an antagonist which the most profound theologian in Europe is wholly unable to overcome.
42. There is not the least use in preaching to anyone unless you chance to catch them ill.
43. What a man that would be had he . . . the least knowledge of the value of red tape.
44. What a mystery is the folly and stupidity of the good!
45. What a pity it is that we have no amusements in England but vice and religion.
46. When a man is a fool, in England we only trust him with the immortal concerns of human beings.
47. When I am in the pulpit, I have the pleasure of seeing my audience nod approbation while they sleep.
48. When I hear any man talk of an unalterable law, I am convinced that he is an unalterable fool.
49. When I take a gun in hand, the safest place for a pheasant is just opposite the muzzle.
50. Whenever I enter a village, straightway I find an ass.
51. The whole of my life has passed like a razor—in hot water or a scrape.
52. You and I are exceptions to the laws of nature; you have risen by your gravity, and I have sunk by my levity.

SMOLLETT, Tobias George, 1721–1771, *English novelist.*

1. He was formed for the ruin of our sex.
2. The painful ceremony of receiving and returning visits.
3. A seafaring man may have a sweetheart in every port; but he should steer clear of a wife as he would avoid a quicksand.
4. Some folks are wise and some are otherwise.

SOCRATES, 470–339 B.C., *Greek philosopher.*

1. As to marriage or celibacy, let a man take which course he will, he will be sure to repent.
2. By all means marry; if you get a good wife, you'll become happy; if you get a bad one, you'll become a philosopher.
3. Call no man unhappy until he is married.
4. Once made equal to man, woman becomes his superior.

SOUSA, John Philip, 1854–1932
American bandmaster and composer.

Jazz will endure just as long as people hear it through their feet instead of their brains.

SPENCER, Herbert, 1820–1903, *English philosopher.*

1. A jury is a group of twelve people of average ignorance.
2. Marriage: a ceremony in which rings are put on the finger of the lady and through the nose of the gentleman.
3. The saying that beauty is but skin-deep is but a skin-deep saying.
4. To play billiards well is a sign of a mis-spent youth.
5. The ultimate result of shielding men from the effects of folly is to fill the world with fools.
6. Volumes might be written on the impiety of the pious.

SPURGEON, Charles Haddon, 1834–1892
English Baptist Minister.

1. Alteration is not always improvement, as the pigeon said when it got out of the net and into the pie.
2. Beware of a mule's hind foot, a dog's tooth, and a woman's tongue.
3. Feel for others—in your pocket.
4. Some ministers would make good martyrs: they are so dry they would burn well.
5. They promise mountains and perform molehills.
6. Train your child in the way you now know you should have gone yourself.

SQUIRE, Sir John, 1884–1958
English poet, essayist, and critic.

1. I'm not so think as you drunk I am.
2. Nothing stales like modernity.

STAËL, Madame de, 1766–1817
French social leader and writer.

1. I am glad I am not a man, for if I were I should be obliged to marry a woman.

2. Love is the history of a woman's life; it is an episode in man's.
3. The more I see of men, the more I like dogs.

STEELE, Richard, 1672–1729, *Irish essayist and playwright.*

1. Ceremony is the invention of wise men to keep fools at a distance.
2. Good breeding is an expedient to make fools and wise men equals.
3. We were . . . fixed in our seats, and sat with that dislike which people not too good-natured conceive of each other at first sight.
4. What's the first excellence in a lawyer? Tautology. What the second? Tautology. What the third? Tautology.
5. A woman seldom writes her mind but in her postscript.

STEINBECK, John, 1902–1968, *American novelist.*

Coney Island: where the surf is one third water and two thirds people.

STENDHAL, 1783–1842

Pen-name of Marie Henri Beyle, French novelist, critic, and biographer.

1. All religions are founded on the fear of the many and the cleverness of the few.
2. Life is too short, and the time we waste in yawning never can be regained.
3. The only excuse for God is that he doesn't exist.
4. The shepherd always tries to persuade the sheep that their interests and his own are the same.

STEPHEN, Sir Leslie, 1832–1904

English editor and man of letters.

Philistine—a term of contempt applied by prigs to the rest of their species.

STEPHENS, James, 1882–1950, *Irish poet and novelist.*

1. Sleep is an excellent way of listening to an opera.
2. Women are wiser than men because they know less and understand more.

STERNE, Laurence, 1713–1768

English novelist and clergyman.

1. Had God thought that sin would enter Eden, He would have created a parson also.
2. Men tire themselves in pursuit of rest.
3. Of all the cants which are canted in this canting world, though the cant of hypocrites may be the worst, the cant of criticism is the most tormenting.
4. There are worse occupations in this world than feeling a woman's pulse.
5. 'Tis known by the name of perseverance in a good cause, and obstinacy in a bad one.
6. Women are timid, and 'tis well they are—else there would be no dealing with them.

STEVENSON, Robert Louis, 1850–1894

Scottish novelist, essayist, and poet.

1. Every man has a sane spot somewhere.
2. Everyone lives by selling something.
3. Give me the young man who has brains enough to make a fool of himself.
4. He sows hurry and reaps indigestion.
5. I have always suspected public taste to be a mongrel product, out of affectation by dogmatism.
6. I've a grand memory for forgetting.
7. If God would give thee grace to see yoursel' the way that ithers see ye, ye would throw your dinner up.
8. If they only married when they fell in love most people would die unwed.
9. If we take matrimony at its lowest, we regard it as a sort of friendship recognized by the police.
10. If your morals make you dreary, depend on it they are wrong.
11. Man is a creature who lives not upon bread alone, but principally by catchwords.
12. Marriage is one long conversation, chequered by disputes.
13. Politics is perhaps the only profession for which no preparation is thought necessary.
14. There is no duty we so much underrate as the duty of being happy.

15. There is nothing more certain than that age and youth are right, except perhaps that both are wrong.
16. Vanity dies hard; in some obstinate cases it outlives the man.
17. What is conscience to a wife? . . . To marry is to domesticate the Recording Angel.

STRACHEY, Lionel, 1864–1927
British writer, translator, and humorist.

1. Any woman in the world, even a nun, would rather lose her virtue than her reputation.
2. A brilliant epigram is a solemn platitude gone to a masquerade ball.
3. Statistics are mendacious truths.
4. To be patriotic, hate all nations but your own; to be religious, all sects but your own; to be moral, all pretences but your own.
5. When humour is meant to be taken seriously, it's no joke.
6. Who says marriage is a failure? It's nothing of the kind—provided you let it alone.

STRUNSKY, Simeon, 1879–1948
American editor, essayist, and author.

The thing which in the subway is called congestion is highly esteemed in the night spots as intimacy.

SURTEES, Robert Smith, 1803–1864, *English novelist.*

1. He had a tremendous determination of words to the mouth.
2. He was a gentleman who was generally spoken of as having nothing a year, paid quarterly.
3. I feels all over trembulation and fear, like a maid that thinks she's not a'goin' to be married.
4. When . . . they rose to go to bed, it struck each man, as he followed his neighbour upstairs, that the one before him walked very crookedly.

SUTRO, Alfred, 1863–1933, *English dramatist.*

My feelings at the moment could only be expressed in camera.

SWIFT, Jonathan, 1667–1745

English satirist, divine, and man of letters.

1. Argument is the worst sort of conversation.
2. Augustus, meeting an ass with a lucky name, foretold himself good fortune; I meet many asses but none of them have lucky names.
3. Better belly burst than good liquor be lost.
4. Censure is the tax a man pays to the public for being eminent.
5. Coming! Ay, so is Christmas.
6. Complaint is the largest tribute heaven receives and the sincerest part of our devotion.
7. A dead wife under the table is the best goods in a man's house.
8. Elephants are always drawn smaller than life, but a flea always larger.
9. Every man desires to live long, but no man would be old.
10. Faith, that's as well said as if I had said it myself.
11. Fine words! I wonder where you stole 'em.
12. Fish should swim thrice: first it should swim in the sea . . . then it should swim in butter, and at last, sirrah, it should swim in good claret.
13. Good God! What a genius I had when I wrote that book.
14. The greatest advantage I know of being thought a wit by the world is that it gives one the greater freedom of playing the fool.
15. Happiness is the perpetual possession of being well deceived.
16. He was an ingenious man that first found out eating and drinking.
17. How is it possible to expect mankind to take advice when they will not so much as take warning?
18. I always like to begin a journey on Sundays because I shall have the prayers of the church to preserve all that travel by land or by water.
19. I'm as old as my tongue and a little older than my teeth.
20. I must complain the cards are ill shuffled till I have a good hand.

21. I never knew any man in my life who could not bear another's misfortune perfectly like a Christian.
22. If a man makes me keep my distance, the comfort is he keeps his at the same time.
23. If a man will observe as he walks in the streets, I believe he will find the merriest countenance in mourning coaches.
24. If Heaven had looked upon riches to be a valuable thing, it would not have given them to such a scoundrel.
25. It is a miserable thing to live in suspense; it is the life of a spider.
26. It is useless for us to attempt to reason a man out of a thing he has never been reasoned into.
27. It is with narrow-souled people as with narrow-necked bottles: the less they have in them, the more noise they make in pouring it out.
28. Last week I saw a woman flayed, and you will hardly believe how much it altered her person for the worse.
29. The latter part of a wise man's life is taken up in curing the follies, prejudices, and false opinions he had contracted in the former.
30. The longer we live the more we should be convinced that it is reasonable to love God and despise man.
31. Lord, I wonder what fool it was that first invented kissing.
32. Love of flattery, in most men, proceeds from the mean opinion they have of themselves; in women from the contrary.
33. A man of business may talk of philosophy, a man who has none may practise it.
34. May you live all the days of your life.
35. My stomach serves me instead of a clock.
36. A nice man is a man of nasty ideas.
37. No man will take counsel, but every man will take money therefore, money is better than counsel.
38. 'Now we are even', quoth Stephen, when he gave his wife six blows for one.
39. Promises and piecrust are made to be broken.
40. Punning is a talent which no man affects to despise but he that is without it.

41. The reason why so few marriages are happy is because young ladies spend their time in making nets, not in making cages.
42. Satire is a sort of glass wherein beholders do generally discover everybody's face but their own.
43. She wears her clothes as if they were thrown on her with a pitchfork.
44. Taverns are places where madness is sold by the bottle.
45. There are few wild beasts more to be dreaded than a talking man having nothing to say.
46. There is nothing in this world constant but inconstancy.
47. Thou hast a head, and so has a pin.
48. 'Tis very warm weather when one's in bed.
49. The two maxims of any great man at court are—always to keep his countenance and never to keep his word.
50. Two women seldom grow intimate but at the expense of a third person.
51. Venus, a beautiful good-natured lady, was the goddess of love; Juno, a terrible shrew, the goddess of marriage; and they were always mortal enemies.
52. A very little wit is valued in a woman, as we are pleased with a few words spoken plain by a parrot.
53. We are so fond of one another because our ailments are the same.
54. We have just enough religion to make us hate but not enough to make us love one another.
55. What religion is he of? Why, he is an Anythingarian.
56. What they do in heaven, we are ignorant of; what they do not, we are told expressly: they neither marry nor are given in marriage.
57. When a true genius appears in the world you may know him by this sign, that the dunces are all in confederacy against him.
58. When men grow virtuous in their old age, they only make a sacrifice to God of the devil's leavings.
59. When you have done a fault, be always pert and insolent, and behave yourself as if you were the injured person.
60. Wit in conversation is, in the midwives' phrase, a quick conception and an easy delivery.

SWINBURNE, Algernon Charles, 1837–1907, *English poet.*

When I hear that a personal friend has fallen into matrimonial courses, I feel the same sorrow as if I had heard of his lapsing into theism.

TAFT, William Howard, 1857–1930

President of the United States and Chief Justice of U.S. Supreme Court.

Some men are graduated from college *cum laude*, some are graduated *summa cum laude*, and some are graduated *mirabile dictu.*

TALLEYRAND, Charles Maurice de, 1754–1838

French statesman and diplomat.

1. A court is an assembly of noble and distinguished beggars.
2. Don't trust first impulses—they are always good.
3. He thinks he is deaf because he no longer hears himself talked about.
4. If you wish to appear agreeable in society, you must consent to be taught many things which you know already.
5. In order to avoid being called a flirt, she always yielded easily.
6. It is worse than a crime, it is a blunder.
7. Never speak ill of yourself; your friends will always say enough on that subject.
8. Only a man who has loved a woman of genius can appreciate what happiness there is in loving a fool.
9. She is intolerable, but that is her only fault.
10. Such a good friend that she will throw all her acquaintances into the water for the pleasure of fishing them out again.
11. What I have been taught, I have forgotten; what I know, I have guessed.

TARKINGTON, Booth, 1869–1946

American novelist and playwright.

1. An ideal wife is any woman who has an ideal husband.
2. The only good in pretending is the fun we get out of fooling ourselves that we fool somebody.

3. There are two things that will be believed of any man whatsoever, and one of them is that he has taken to drink.

TAVERNER, Richard, 1505?–1577, *English religious reformer.*

Wedded persons may thus pass over their lives quietly . . . if the husband becomes deaf and the wife blind.

TAYLOR, Jeremy, 1613–1667
English bishop and religious writer.

Better to sit up all night than go to bed with a dragon.

TENNYSON, Alfred, Lord, 1809–1892, *English poet.*

1. Charm us, orator, till the lion look no larger than the cat.
2. The curate—he was fatter than his cure.

TERENCE, 190?–159? B.C., *Roman poet and dramatist.*

1. I should like to see your head stroked with a sandal.
2. She never was really charming till she died.
3. There is a demand nowadays for men who can make wrong appear right.
4. There is nothing that can't be made worse by telling.

THACKERAY, William Makepeace, 1811–1863
English novelist.

1. A clever, ugly man every now and then is successful with the ladies, but a handsome fool is irresistible.
2. Good humour may be said to be one of the very best articles of dress one can wear in society.
3. He that hath ears to hear, let him stuff them with cotton.
4. If a man's character is to be abused, there's nobody like a relative to do the business.
5. Kindness is very indigestible. It disagrees with very proud stomachs.
6. One man is as good as another—and a great dale betther, as the Irish philosopher said.
7. 'Tis strange what a man may do, and a woman yet think him an angel.
8. To love and win is the best thing; to love and lose, the next best.

7

9. When I walk with you I feel as if I had a flower in my buttonhole.

THOMAS, Albert Ellsworth, 1872–1847

American playwright.

It takes a major operation to extract money from a minor poet.

THOREAU, Henry David, 1817–1862

American author and naturalist.

1. Any fool can make a rule, and every fool will mind it.
2. Be not simply good; be good for something.
3. Beware of all enterprises that require new clothes.
4. The boy gathers materials for a temple, and then when he is thirty concludes to build a woodshed.
5. City life: millions of people being lonesome together.
6. Every generation laughs at the old fashions, but follows religiously the new.
7. I cannot easily buy a blankbook to write thoughts in; they are commonly ruled for dollars and cents.
8. I have received no more than one or two letters in my life that were worth the postage.
9. I have three chairs in my house: one for solitude, two for friendship, three for company.
10. If I repent of anything, it is very likely to be my good behaviour.
11. If words were invented to conceal thought, newspapers are a great improvement on a bad invention.
12. It is an interesting question how far men would retain their relative rank if they were divested of their clothes.
13. It is not worth while to go round the world to count the cats in Zanzibar.
14. It makes but little difference whether you are committed to a farm or a county jail.
15. A man is rich in proportion to the number of things which he can afford to let alone.
16. The mass of men lead lives of quiet desperation.
17. My dwelling was small, and I could hardly entertain an echo in it.

18. Not that the story need be long, but it will take a long while to make it short.
19. Nothing makes the earth seem so spacious as to have friends at a distance; they make the latitudes and longitudes.
20. The rarest quality in an epitaph is truth.
21. Some circumstantial evidence is very strong, as when you find a trout in the milk.
22. There are nowadays professors of philosophy, but not philosophers.
23. What is commonly called friendship is only a little more honor among rogues.
24. What men call good fellowship is commonly but the virtue of pigs in a litter which lie close together to keep each other warm.

THURBER, James, 1894–1961

American humorous writer and artist.

1. Early to rise and early to bed makes a male healthy and wealthy and dead.
2. He fell down a great deal during his boyhood because of a trick he had of walking into himself.
3. Well, if I called the wrong number, why did you answer the phone?
4. While he was not dumber than an ox, he was not any smarter.

TOLSTOI, Leo Nikolaevich, 1828–1910

Russian novelist, social reformer, and mystic.

1. All happy families are alike, but each unhappy family is unhappy in its own way.
2. He never chooses an opinion; he just wears whatever happens to be in style.
3. He will do almost anything for the poor, except get off their backs.

TOSCANINI, Arturo, 1867–1957

Italian operatic and symphonic conductor.

I kissed my first woman and smoked my first cigarette on the same day; I have never had time for tobacco since.

TREE, Sir Herbert Beerbohm, 1853–1917

English actor and theatrical manager.

A man never knows what a fool he is until he hears himself imitated by one.

TROLLOPE, Anthony, 1815–1882, *English novelist.*

The best right a woman has is the right to a husband.

TWAIN, Mark, 1835–1910

Pen-name of Samuel Langhorne Clemens, American humorous writer and wit.

1. Adam and Eve had many advantages, but the principal one was that they escaped teething.
2. Adam was human; he didn't want the apple for the apple's sake; he wanted it because it was forbidden.
3. All religions issue Bibles against Satan, and say the most injurious things against him, but we never hear his side.
4. All that I care to know is that a man is a human being—that is enough for me; he can't be any worse.
5. All you need in this life is ignorance and confidence, and then success is sure.
6. Always do right; this will gratify some people and astonish the rest.
7. Animals talk to each other; I never knew but one man who could understand them—I knew he could because he told me so himself.
8. April 1 is the day upon which we are reminded of what we are on the other 364.
9. A banker is a fellow who lends you his umbrella when the sun is shining and wants it back the minute it begins to rain.
10. Barring that natural expression of villainy which we all have, the man looked honest enough.
11. Be good and you will be lonesome.
12. Be virtuous and you will be eccentric.
13. By trying we can easily learn to endure adversity—another man's I mean.
14. A classic is something that everybody wants to have read and nobody wants to read.

15. The Creator made Italy from designs by Michelangelo.
16. The emperor sent his troops to the field with immense enthusiasm; he will lead them in person—when they return.
17. The English are mentioned in the Bible: Blessed are the meek, for they shall inherit the earth.
18. Everybody was sorry she died; but I reckoned with her disposition—she was having a better time in the graveyard.
19. Familiarity breeds contempt—and children.
20. Few things are harder to put up with than the annoyance of a good example.
21. The first half of life consists of the capacity to enjoy without the chance; the last half consists of the chance without the capacity.
22. Get your facts first, and then you can distort them as much as you please.
23. Good breeding consists in concealing how much we think of ourselves and how little we think of the other person.
24. A good memory and a tongue tied in the middle is a combination which gives immortality to conversation.
25. Hain't we got all the fools in town on our side, and ain't that a big enough majority in any town?
26. Have a place for everything and keep the thing somewhere else; this is not advice, it is merely custom.
27. Heaven goes by favour; if it went by merit, you would stay out and your dog would go in.
28. He charged nothing for his preaching, and it was worth it, too.
29. He has been a doctor a year now and has had two patients—no, three, I think—yes, it was three; I attended their funerals.
30. He liked to like people, therefore people liked him.
31. He was a very inferior farmer when he first began, and he is now fast rising from affluence to poverty.
32. His money is twice tainted: 'taint yours and 'taint mine.
33. The holy passion of friendship is of so sweet and steady and loyal and enduring a nature that it will last through a whole life-time, if not asked to lend money.

34. Honest poverty is a gem that even a king might be proud to call his own, but I wish to sell out.
35. The human race consists of the dangerously insane and such as are not.
36. I am an old man and have known a great many troubles, but most of them never happened.
37. I could never learn to like her—except on a raft at sea with no other provisions in sight.
38. I don't give a damn for a man that can spell a word only one way.
39. I have been an author for twenty-two years and an ass for fifty-five.
40. I have never let my schooling interfere with my education.
41. I like criticism, but it must be my way.
42. If you pick up a starving dog and make him prosperous, he will not bite you; that is the principal difference between a dog and a man.
43. If you tell the truth, you don't have to remember anything.
44. In all matters of opinion, our adversaries are insane.
45. In all my travels the thing that has impressed me the most is the universal brotherhood of man—what there is of it.
46. In our country we have those three unspeakably precious things: freedom of speech, freedom of conscience, and the prudence never to practice either.
47. In statesmanship, get the formalities right; never mind about the moralities.
48. It has always been my rule never to smoke when asleep, and never to refrain when awake.
49. It is a difference of opinion that makes horse races.
50. It seems such a pity that Noah and his party did not miss the boat.
51. It usually takes me more than three weeks to prepare a good impromptu speech.
52. It was wonderful to find America, but it would have been more wonderful to miss it.
53. It would have been foolish to stand upon our dignity in a place where there was hardly room to stand upon our feet.
54. Let us be thankful for the fools; but for them the rest of us could not succeed.

55. Let us endeavour so to live that when we come to die even the undertaker will be sorry.
56. Let us not be too particular; it is better to have old second-hand diamonds than none at all.
57. A man is accepted into a church for what he believes and he is turned out for what he knows.
58. Man is the only animal that blushes—or needs to.
59. Man was made at the end of the week's work when God was tired.
60. The man who can't tell a lie thinks he is the best judge of one.
61. The man who is a pessimist before forty-eight knows too much; the man who is an optimist after forty-eight knows too little.
62. The moral sense enables one to perceive morality—and avoid it; the immoral sense enables one to perceive immorality—and enjoy it.
63. Most writers regard truth as their most valuable possession, and therefore are most economical in its use.
64. Nothing so needs reforming as other people's habits.
65. The older we grow the greater becomes our wonder at how much ignorance one can contain without bursting one's clothes.
66. The only way to keep your health is to eat what you don't want, drink what you don't like, and do what you'd rather not.
67. Our Heavenly Father invented man because he was disappointed in the monkey.
68. Part of the secret of success in life is to eat what you like and let the food fight it out inside.
69. Principles have no real force except when one is well fed.
70. Put all your eggs in one basket, and watch the basket.
71. Repartee is something we think of twenty-four hours too late.
72. The reports of my death are greatly exaggerated.
73. The secret source of humor is not joy but sorrow; there is no humor in heaven.
74. Soap and education are not as sudden as a massacre, but they are more deadly in the long run.

75. There are many humorous things in the world: among them the white man's notion that he is less savage than the other savages.
76. There are many scapegoats for our sins, but the most popular is Providence.
77. There are no people who are quite so vulgar as the over-refined ones.
78. There are several good protections against temptation, but the surest is cowardice.
79. There are two times in a man's life when he should not speculate: when he can't afford it, and when he can.
80. There is a lot to say in her favor, but the other is more interesting.
81. There is no use in walking five miles to fish when you can depend on being just as unsuccessful near home.
82. There's always something about your success that displeases even your best friends.
83. They spell it Vinci and pronounce it Vinchy; foreigners always spell better than they pronounce.
84. To be good is noble, but to teach others how to be good is nobler—and less trouble.
85. To cease smoking is the easiest thing I ever did; I ought to know because I've done it a thousand times.
86. To create man was a fine and original idea; but to add the sheep was a tautology.
87. To eat is human; to digest, divine.
88. Training is everything: the peach was once a bitter almond; cauliflower is nothing but cabbage with a college education.
89. Truth is stranger than fiction; fiction is obliged to stick to possibilities, truth isn't.
90. Virtue has never been as respectable as money.
91. Wagner's music is better than it sounds.
92. Water, taken in moderation, cannot hurt anybody.
93. We do not deal much in facts when we are contemplating ourselves.
94. We owe a deep debt of gratitude to Adam, the first great benefactor of the human race: he brought death into the world.

95. What a good thing Adam had—when he said a good thing, he knew nobody had said it before.
96. What a man misses mostly in heaven is company.
97. What is the difference between a taxidermist and a tax collector? The taxidermist takes only your skin.
98. Whatever a man's age, he can reduce it several years by putting a bright-colored flower in his buttonhole.
99. When a man's dog turns against him it is time for a wife to pack her trunk and go home to mama.
100. When I reflect upon the number of disagreeable people who I know have gone to a better world, I am moved to lead a different life.
101. When I speak my native tongue in its utmost purity in England, an Englishman can't understand me at all.
102. When in doubt, tell the truth.
103. When some men discharge an obligation you can hear the report for miles around.
104. Why is it that we rejoice at a birth and grieve at a funeral? Is it because we are not the person concerned?

TYRRELL, George, 1861–1909, *Irish theologian.*
The *reductio ad absurdum* is God's favourite argument.

UNDSET, Sigrid, 1882–1949, *Norwegian novelist.*
He was not made for climbing the tree of knowledge.

VICTORIA, Queen of England, 1819–1901
He speaks to me as if I were a public meeting.

VOLTAIRE, 1694–1778
Pen-name of François Marie Arouet, French political philosopher, historian, satirist, dramatist, essayist, and novelist.

1. Animals have these advantages over man: they have no theologians to instruct them, their funerals cost them nothing, and no one starts lawsuits over their wills.
2. The art of government consists in taking as much money as possible from one class of citizens to give to the other.

3. The art of medicine consists of amusing the patient while nature cures the disease.
4. A clergyman is one who feels himself called upon to live without working at the expense of the rascals who work to live.
5. Common sense is not so common.
6. Divorce dates from just about the same time as marriage; I think that marriage is a few weeks older.
7. Doctors pour drugs of which they know little, to cure diseases of which they know less, into human beings of whom they know nothing.
8. England has forty-two religions and only two sauces.
9. An Englishman, like a free man, goes to heaven by the way which pleases him.
10. Every species of mankind is good except the bore species.
11. The fate of a nation has often depended upon the good or bad digestion of a prime minister.
12. God created woman only to tame man.
13. Heaven made virtue; man, its appearance.
14. The Holy Roman Empire was neither holy, nor Roman, nor an empire.
15. The husband who desires to surprise is often very much surprised himself.
16. Ideas are like beards: men do not have them until they grow up.
17. I know I am among civilized men because they are fighting so savagely.
18. I was never ruined but twice: once when I lost a lawsuit, and once when I won one.
19. If God did not exist, it would be necessary to invent Him.
20. Illusion is the first of all pleasures.
21. In the great game of human life one begins by being a dupe and ends by being a rogue.
22. The infinitely little have pride infinitely great.
23. Marriage is the only adventure open to the cowardly.
24. The multitude of books is making us ignorant.
25. My life's dream has been a perpetual nightmare.
26. My prayer to God is a very short one: 'O Lord, make my enemies most ridiculous!' God has granted it.

27. Originality is nothing but judicious imitation.
28. The punishment of criminals should be of use: when a man is hanged he is good for nothing.
29. Satire lies about literary men while they live, and eulogy lies about them when they die.
30. The secret of being a bore is to tell everything.
31. The superfluous: a very necessary thing.
32. To forgive our enemies their virtues—that is a greater miracle.
33. We use ideas merely to justify our evil, and speech merely to conceal our ideas.
34. When he who hears doesn't know what he who speaks means, and when he who speaks doesn't know what he himself means—that is philosophy.
35. When it is a question of money, everybody is of the same religion.
36. A woman can keep one secret—the secret of her age.

VORSE, Mary Heaton, 1898–1966

American short-story writer, author, and social reformer.

The art of writing is the art of applying the seat of the pants to the seat of the chair.

WADE, Harry V., born 1894

American newspaperman and comic columnist, creator of 'Senator Soaper'.

1. Aziz Ezzet, a gentleman of importance in Egypt, says his name can be pronounced by opening a soda bottle slowly.
2. Gypsy Rose Lee, the strip-tease artist, has arrived in Hollywood with twelve empty trunks.
3. The ideal voice for radio may be defined as having no substance, no sex, no owner, and a message of importance to every house-wife.
4. Paragraphing is one of the lower forms of cunning, like a way with women.
5. Though General Sherman lived on into the peace, he never said what he thought of it.
6. Youth today must be strong, unafraid, and a better taxpayer than its father.

WALKER, James J., 1881–1946, *American politician.*

1. If you're there before it's over, you're on time.
2. A reformer is a man who rides through a sewer in a glass-bottomed boat.

WALKER, Stanley, 1898–1962
American journalist and author.

He was an author whose works were so little known as to be almost confidential.

WALLACE, Edgar, 1875–1932, *English novelist and playwright.*

1. There is so much nastiness in modern literature that I like to write stories which contain nothing worse than a little innocent murdering.
2. What is a highbrow? He is a man who has found something more interesting than women.

WALPOLE, Horace, 1717–1797
English author, letter writer, and antiquarian.

1. Art and life ought to be hurriedly remarried and brought to live together.
2. Every drop of ink in my pen ran cold.
3. I never knew but one woman who would not take gold—and she took diamonds.
4. I never understand anything until I have written about it.
5. I should like my country well enough, if it were not for my countrymen.
6. In my youth I thought of writing a satire on mankind but now in my age I think I should write an apology for them.
7. The newspapers have given the rage of going to Paris a good name: they call it the French disease.
8. Spring has set in with its usual severity.
9. There are playthings for all ages; the playthings of old people is to talk of the playthings of their youth.
10. The way to ensure summer in England is to have it framed and glazed in a comfortable room.
11. We are now so badly degenerated that three Frenchmen can evidently beat one Englishman.
12. The wisest prophets make sure of the event first.

WALTON, Izaak, 1593–1683, *English author and biographer.*

1. Every misery I miss is a new blessing.
2. That which is everybody's business is nobody's business.

WARBURTON, William, 1698–1779, *English divine.*

Orthodoxy is my doxy; heterodoxy is another man's doxy.

WARD, Artemus, 1834–1867

Pen-name of Charles Farrar Browne, American humorist.

1. Alas, she married another; they frequently do; I hope she is happy—because I am.
2. By a sudden and adroit movement I placed my left eye against his fist.
3. Did you ever have the measles, and if so, how many?
4. The female woman is one of the greatest institutions of which this land can boast.
5. The ground flew up and hit me in the head.
6. I am not a politician, and my other habits are good.
7. I am saddest when I sing; so are those who hear me; they are sadder even than I am.
8. I have already given two cousins to the war, and I stand ready to sacrifice my wife's brother.
9. I have no politics—nary a one.
10. I now bid you a welcome adieu.
11. I prefer temperance hotels, although they sell worse liquor than any other kind of hotels.
12. I wish there was windows to my soul, so that you could see some of my feelings.
13. It is a pity that Chawcer, who had geneyus, was so unedicated; he's the wuss speller I know of.
14. Let us all be happy and live within our means, even if we have to borrow the money to do it with.
15. The Mormon's religion is singular, and his wives are plural.
16. One of the principal features of my entertainment is that it contains so many things that don't have anything to do with it.

17. Shakespeare endorses polygamy: he speaks of the Merry Wives of Windsor; how many wives did Mr. Windsor have?
18. There's a good deal of human nature in man.
19. They drink with impunity, or anybody who invites them.
20. Thrice is he armed that hath his quarrel just—and four times he who gets his fist in fust.
21. Why care for grammar as long as we are good?
22. Why is this thus? What is the reason of this thusness?

WARNER, Charles Dudley, 1829–1900
American editor and essayist.

1. Blessed be agriculture—if one does not have too much of it.
2. Everybody talks about the weather but nobody does anything about it.
3. Nothing can move a man who is paid by the hour; how sweet the flight of time seems to his calm mind.
4. One of the best things in the world to be is a boy; it requires no experience, but needs some practice to be a good one.
5. There is but one pleasure in life equal to that of being called on to make an after-dinner speech, and that is not being called on to make one.
6. The thing generally raised on city land is taxes.
7. What a man needs in gardening is a cast-iron back, with a hinge in it.

WARNER, Sylvia Townsend, born 1893, *English novelist.*

There had been no leisure in his life, there had only been holidays.

WELLES, Orson, born 1915
American actor, director, and producer of motion pictures, radio, and stage.

1. I don't say we all ought to misbehave, but we ought to look as if we could.
2. Now we sit through Shakespeare in order to recognize the quotations.
3. When you're down and out, something always turns up—and it's usually the noses of your friends.

WELLINGTON, Duke of, 1769–1852

English soldier and politician.

I don't care a twopenny damn what becomes of the ashes of Napoleon.

WELLS, Carolyn, 187–?–1942

American humorous and voluminous writer.

1. Actions lie louder than words.
2. At times there is nothing so unnatural as nature.
3. A blunder at the right moment is better than cleverness at the wrong time.
4. Charity uncovers a multitude of sins.
5. Circumstances alter faces.
6. A critic is a necessary evil, and criticism is an evil necessity.
7. A cynic is a man who looks at the world with a monocle in his mind's eye.
8. Dead men sell no tales.
9. Epigrams cover a multitude of sins.
10. Every dogma must have its day.
11. A guilty conscience is the mother of invention.
12. He who loves and runs away may live to love another day.
13. It's a wise child that owes his own father.
14. Man's importunity is woman's opportunity.
15. Of two evils choose the prettier.
16. One man's fish is another man's *poisson*.
17. The wages of sin is alimony.
18. We should live and learn; but by the time we've learned, it's too late to live.

WELLS, Herbert George, 1866–1946

English novelist, short-story writer, historian, and sociologist.

1. Every time Europe looks across the Atlantic to see the American eagle, it observes only the rear end of an ostrich.
2. His studies were pursued but never effectually overtaken.
3. 'I'm a Norfan, both sides', he would explain, with an air of one who has seen trouble.
4. Moral indignation is jealousy with a halo.

5. She had a lot of fat that did not fit.
6. What on earth would a man do with himself if something did not stand in his way?

WEST, Rebecca, born 1892, *English novelist and critic.*

1. He is every other inch a gentleman.
2. He makes that insistence on privacy which is the perverse demand of those surfeited with public admiration.
3. It is a thankless task to be the perfect embodiment of a transition period.
4. One could imagine her giving Pavlova a few hints on dancing because she had been such a success as a skirt-dancer at bazaars in her youth.
5. She is, past all possibility of cure, a woman novelist.

WESTCOTT, Edward Noyes, 1846–1898
American banker and novelist.

A reasonable amount of fleas is good for a dog; it keeps him from brooding over being a dog.

WHATELY, Richard, 1787–1863, *English scholar and prelate.*

1. Happiness is no laughing matter.
2. Honesty is the best policy, but he who is governed by that maxim is not an honest man.
3. It is a folly to expect men to do all that they may reasonably be expected to do.
4. Never argue at the dinner table, for the one who is not hungry always gets the best of the argument.
5. Party spirit enlists a man's virtues in the cause of his vices.

WHEATLEY, Henry Benjamin, 1838–1917
English bibliographer and scholar.

We usually call our blunders mistakes, and our friends style our mistakes blunders.

WHISTLER, James McNeill, 1834–1903
Anglo-American painter and etcher.

1. An artist's career always begins tomorrow.

2. I'm lonesome. They are all dying. I have hardly a warm personal enemy left.
3. Nature is usually wrong.

WHITE, William Allen, 1868–1944
American journalist and author.

My advice to the women's clubs of America is to raise more hell and fewer dahlias.

WHITMAN, Walt, 1819–1892, *American poet.*

1. The Americans, like the English, probably make love worse than any other race.
2. Damn all expurgated books; the dirtiest book of all is the expurgated book.
3. I am as bad as the worst but, thank God, I am as good as the best.
4. I find no sweeter fat than sticks to my own bones.

WILDE, Oscar, 1856–1900, *British dramatist and poet.*

1. The advantage of the emotions is that they lead us astray.
2. After a good dinner, one can forgive anybody, even one's own relatives.
3. Alas, I am dying beyond my means.
4. All charming people are spoiled; it is the secret of their attraction.
5. All women become like their mothers—that is their tragedy; no man does—that's his.
6. Ambition is the last refuge of the failure.
7. Anybody can be good in the country; there are no temptations there.
8. Anybody can make history; only a great man can write it.
9. Anyone can sympathize with the sufferings of a friend, but it requires a very fine nature to sympathize with a friend's success.
10. Arguments are extremely vulgar, for everybody in good society holds exactly the same opinions.
11. Arguments are to be avoided; they are always vulgar and often convincing.

12. As long as a woman can look ten years younger than her own daughter, she is perfectly satisfied.
13. As soon as people are old enough to know better, they don't know anything at all.
14. Bad manners make a journalist.
15. Being natural is simply a pose.
16. Bernard Shaw is an excellent man; he has not an enemy in the world, and none of his friends like him.
17. The best way to make children is to make them happy.
18. A bishop keeps on saying at the age of eighty what he was told to say when he was a boy of eighteen.
19. The Book of Life begins with a man and a woman in a garden, and it ends with Revelations.
20. Books of poetry by young writers are usually promissory notes that are never met.
21. The books that the world calls immoral are books that show the world its own shame.
22. By persistently remaining single, a man converts himself into a permanent public temptation.
23. Caricature is the tribute that mediocrity pays to genius.
24. Charity creates a multitude of sins.
25. Children begin by loving their parents; after a time they judge them. Rarely if ever they forgive them.
26. Clever people never listen and stupid people never talk.
27. Conscience makes egotists of us all.
28. Consistency is the last refuge of the unimaginative.
29. Crying is the refuge of plain women, but the ruin of pretty ones.
30. Democracy means simply the bludgeoning of the people, by the people, for the people.
31. The difference between literature and journalism is that journalism is unreadable and literature is unread.
32. Divorces are made in heaven.
33. Don't be misled into the paths of virtue.
34. Duty is what one expects from others.
35. English actors act quite well, but they act best between the lines.
36. The English country gentleman galloping after a fox—the unspeakable in full pursuit of the uneatable.

37. The English have a miraculous power of turning wine into water.
38. The English public takes no interest in a work of art until it is told that the work in question is immoral.
39. Everybody who is incapable of learning has taken to teaching.
40. Everyone should keep someone else's diary.
41. Experience is simply the name we give our mistakes.
42. Fashion is a form of ugliness so intolerable that we have to alter it every six months.
43. Fashion is that by which the fantastic becomes for a moment universal.
44. Fashion is what one wears oneself: what is unfashionable is what other people wear.
45. The fatality of good resolutions is that they are always too late.
46. Fathers should be neither seen nor heard; that is the only proper basis for family life.
47. Few parents nowadays pay any regard to what their children say to them; the old-fashioned respect for the young is fast dying out.
48. The first duty in life is to be as artificial as possible; what the second duty is, no one has yet discovered.
49. Flowers are as common in the country as people are in London.
50. Frank Harris is invited to all the great houses in England—once.
51. Genius is born, not paid.
52. A gentleman is one who never hurts anyone's feelings unintentionally.
53. George Moore wrote brilliant English until he discovered grammar.
54. The good end happily, the bad unhappily—that is what fiction means.
55. The happiness of a married man depends on the people he has not married.
56. He doesn't act on the stage—he behaves.
57. He had the sort of face that, once seen, is never remembered.

58. He hasn't a single redeeming vice.
59. He is old enough to know worse.
60. He knew the precise psychological moment when to say nothing.
61. He was always late on principle, his principle being that punctuality is the thief of time.
62. Henry James writes fiction as if it were a painful duty.
63. Her capacity for family affection is extraordinary; when her third husband died, her hair turned quite gold from grief.
64. I beg your pardon, I didn't recognize you—I've changed a lot.
65. I can believe anything—provided it is incredible.
66. I can resist everything except temptation.
67. I choose my friends for their good looks, my acquaintances for their good characters, and my enemies for their good intellects.
68. I do not approve of anything which tampers with natural ignorance.
69. I do not play cricket because it requires me to assume such indecent postures.
70. I like men who have a future and women who have a past.
71. I like Wagner's music better than anybody's; it is so loud, one can talk the whole time without other people hearing what one says.
72. I must decline your invitation owing to a subsequent engagement.
73. I never put off till tomorrow what I can possibly do the day after.
74. If a woman wants to hold a man she has only to appeal to what is worst in him.
75. If one could only teach the English how to talk and the Irish how to listen, society would be quite civilized.
76. If one hears bad music it is one's duty to drown it in conversation.
77. If one plays good music, people don't listen; if one plays bad music, people don't talk.
78. If one tells the truth, one is sure sooner or later to be found out.

79. If the lower orders don't set us a good example, what on earth is the use of them?
80. Ignorance is like a delicate exotic fruit: touch it, and the bloom is gone.
81. In America, the President reigns for four years, and journalism governs for ever and ever.
82. In America, the young are always ready to give to those who are older than themselves the full benefits of their inexperience.
83. In examinations the foolish ask questions that the wise cannot answer.
84. In love, one always begins by deceiving oneself, and one always ends by deceiving others; that is what the world calls a romance.
85. In married life, three is company and two none.
86. In the old days men had the rack; now they have the press.
87. In this world there are only two tragedies: one is not getting what one wants, and the other is getting it.
88. Insincerity is merely a method by which we can multiply our personalities.
89. It is always a silly thing to give advice, but to give good advice is absolutely fatal.
90. It is a terrible thing for a man to find out suddenly that all his life he has been speaking nothing but the truth.
91. It is dangerous to be sincere unless you are also stupid.
92. It is only an auctioneer who should admire all schools of art.
93. It is only by not paying one's bills that one can hope to live in the memory of the commercial classes.
94. It is perfectly monstrous the way people go about nowadays saying things against one, behind one's back, that are absolutely and entirely true.
95. Land gives one position, and prevents one from keeping it up.
96. Laughter is not a bad beginning for a friendship, and it is the best ending for one.
97. Life is far too important a thing ever to talk seriously about.
98. The London season is entirely matrimonial; people are either hunting for husbands or hiding from them.
99. The longer I live the more keenly I feel that whatever was good enough for our fathers is not good enough for us.

100. A man can be happy with any woman as long as he does not love her.
101. A man cannot be too careful in the choice of his enemies.
102. Man is a rational animal who always loses his temper when he is called upon to act in accordance with the dictates of reason.
103. A man who desires to get married should know either everything or nothing.
104. A man who moralizes is usually a hypocrite, and a woman who moralizes is invariably plain.
105. A map of the world that does not include Utopia is not worth glancing at.
106. Marriage is the one subject on which all woman agree and all men disagree.
107. Memory is the diary that we all carry about with us.
108. Men always want to be a woman's first love; women have a more subtle instinct: what they like is to be a man's last romance.
109. Men become old but they never become good.
110. Men marry because they are tired, women because they are curious; both are disappointed.
111. Meredith is a prose Browning, and so is Browning; he used poetry as a medium for writing in prose.
112. Misfortunes one can endure, they come from the outside; but to suffer for one's faults—ah! there is the sting of life.
113. Modern journalism justifies its own existence by the great Darwinian principle of the survival of the vulgarest.
114. Modern women understand everything except their husbands.
115. Morality is simply the attitude we adopt towards people whom we personally dislike.
116. More than half of modern culture depends on what one shouldn't read.
117. More women grow old nowadays through the faithfulness of their admirers than through anything else.
118. Murder is always a mistake; one should never do anything that one cannot talk about after dinner.
119. My own business always bores me to death; I prefer other people's.

120. Never buy a thing you don't want merely because it is dear.

121. No man should have a secret from his wife; she invariably finds it out.

122. No woman should ever be quite accurate about her age—it looks so calculating.

123. Nothing looks so like innocence as an indiscretion.

124. Nothing spoils a romance so much as a sense of humour in the woman.

125. Nothing succeeds like excess.

126. Nowadays all the married men live like bachelors, and all the bachelors live like married men.

127. Nowadays to be intelligible is to be found out.

128. Of course, America had often been discovered before Columbus, but it had always been hushed up.

129. The old believe everything, the middle-aged suspect everything, the young know everything.

130. On an occasion of this kind it becomes more than a moral duty to speak one's mind; it becomes a pleasure.

131. One can always recognize women who trust their husbands; they look so thoroughly unhappy.

132. One can survive everything nowadays except death.

133. The one charm of marriage is that it makes a life of deception absolutely necessary for both parties.

134. One half of the world does not believe in God, and the other half does not believe in me.

135. One man's poetry is another man's poison.

136. One should always be in love; that is the reason one should never marry.

137. One should always play fairly when one has the winning cards.

138. One should never make one's début with a scandal; one should reserve that to give interest to one's old age.

139. One should never trust a woman who tells one her real age; a woman who would tell one that would tell one anything.

140. One should not be too severe on English novels; they are the only relaxation of the intellectually unemployed.

141. One's real life is so often the life that one does not lead.

142. The only difference between a caprice and a lifelong passion is that the caprice lasts a little longer.
143. The only difference between the saint and the sinner is that every saint has a past and every sinner has a future.
144. The only form of lying that is absolutely beyond reproach is lying for its own sake.
145. The only really humanizing influence in prison is the influence of the prisoners.
146. The only thing to do with good advice is to pass it on; it is never of any use to oneself.
147. The only way a woman can ever reform a man is by boring him so completely that he loses all possible interest in life.
148. The only way to behave to a woman is to make love to her if she is pretty and to someone else if she is plain.
149. The only way to get rid of a temptation is to yield to it.
150. Philanthropy is the refuge of people who wish to annoy their fellow creatures.
151. A poet can survive everything but a misprint.
152. Prayer must never be answered; if it is, it ceases to be prayer and becomes a correspondence.
153. The proper basis for marriage is a mutual misunderstanding.
154. The public is wonderfully tolerant—it forgives everything except genius.
155. The public have an insatiable curiosity to know everything—except what is worth knowing.
156. Questions are never indiscreet; answers sometimes are.
157. The real tragedy of the poor is that they can afford nothing but self-denial.
158. A really well-made buttonhole is the only link between art and nature.
159. The reason we are so pleased to find out other people's secrets is that it distracts public attention from our own.
160. Relations are simply a tedious pack of people who haven't got the remotest knowledge of how to live nor the smallest instinct about when to die.
161. She has the remains of really remarkable ugliness.
162. She is a peacock in everything but beauty.

163. She looks like the de luxe edition of a wicked French novel meant especially for the English market.
164. She who hesitates is won.
165. She wore far too much rouge last night and not quite enough clothes; that is always a sign of despair in a woman.
166. Simple pleasures are the last refuge of the complex.
167. Society produces rogues, and education makes one rogue cleverer than another.
168. There are moments when art attains almost to the dignity of manual labour.
169. There are only five women in London worth talking to, and two of these can't be admitted into decent society.
170. There are terrible temptations which it requires strength and courage to yield to.
171. There are two ways of disliking art: one is to dislike it; the other, to like it rationally.
172. There is hardly a person in the House of Commons worth painting, though many of them would be better for a little whitewashing.
173. There is only one class in the community that thinks more about money than the rich, and that is the poor.
174. There is only one thing in the world worse than being talked about, and that is not being talked about.
175. There's nothing in the world like the devotion of a married woman; it's a thing no married man knows anything about.
176. Thirty-five is a very attractive age; London society is full of women who have of their own free choice remained thirty-five for years.
177. Those who are faithless know the pleasures of love; it is the faithful who know love's tragedies.
178. Those who see any difference between soul and body have neither.
179. To expect the unexpected shows a thoroughly modern intellect.
180. To lose one parent may be regarded as a misfortune; to lose both looks like carelessness.
181. To love oneself is the beginning of a lifelong romance.

182. Truly religious people are resigned to everything, even to mediocre poetry.

183. Twenty years of romance make a woman look like a ruin, but twenty years of marriage make her something like a public building.

184. Vulgarity is simply the conduct of others.

185. We have really everything in common with America nowadays except, of course, language.

186. We live in an age when unnecessary things are our only necessities.

187. We think we are generous because we credit our neighbour with the possession of those virtues that are likely to benefit us.

188. A well-tied tie is the first serious step in life.

189. When a woman marries again it is because she detested her first husband; when a man marries again it is because he adored his first wife.

190. When I was young I used to think that money was the most important thing in life; now that I am old, I know it is.

191. When people agree with me I always feel that I must be wrong.

192. When the gods wish to punish us they answer our prayers.

193. Whenever a man does a thoroughly stupid thing, it is always from the noblest motives.

194. Whenever cannibals are on the brink of starvation, Heaven in its infinite mercy sends them a nice plump missionary.

195. Whenever one has anything unpleasant to say, one should always be quite candid.

196. Whistler, with all his faults, was never guilty of writing a line of poetry.

197. Wicked women bother one; good women bore one; that is the only difference between them.

198. With an evening coat and a white tie, anybody, even a stockbroker, can gain a reputation for being civilized.

199. Woman begins by resisting a man's advances and ends by blocking his retreat.

200. A woman with a past has no future.

201. Women are meant to be loved, not to be understood.

202. Women as a sex are sphinxes without secrets.
203. Women have a much better time than men in this world; there are far more things forbidden to them.
204. Women have a wonderful instinct about things; they can discover anything except the obvious.
205. Women have been so highly educated that nothing should surprise them except happy marriages.
206. Women love us for our defects; if we have enough of them they will forgive us everything, even our superior intellects.
207. Women's styles may change but their designs remain the same.
208. Women treat us just as humanity treats its gods; they worship us and are always bothering us to do something for them.
209. The world is a stage, but the play is badly cast.
210. The world is divided into two classes: those who believe the incredible, and those who do the improbable.
211. The world reads too much to be wise and thinks too much to be beautiful.
212. You know what a woman's curiosity is—almost as great as a man's.
213. You should study the Peerage; it is the best thing in fiction the English have ever done.
214. Young men want to be faithful and are not; old men want to be faithless and cannot.
215. The youth of America is their oldest tradition; it has been going on now for three hundred years.

WILDER, Thornton, born 1897
American novelist and playwright.

She's going to make some man a good wife someday, provided he comes down off the movie screen and asks her.

WILSON, Woodrow, 1856–1924, *President of the United States.*

1. All the extraordinary men I have ever known were chiefly extraordinary in their own estimation.
2. A conservative is a man who just sits and thinks, mostly sits.

3. Every man who takes office in Washington either grows or swells.
4. Gossip: sociologists on a mean and petty scale.
5. He is more apt to contribute heat than light to a discussion.
6. Some Americans need hyphens in their name because only part of them has come over.

WINNINGTON, Richard, 1904–1953
English film critic and caricaturist.

1. Anybody who did anything in America up to 1900 is liable to be made into a film . . . on the grounds of being a pioneer.
2. Film studios have evolved a new tongue—the broken accent to be used by all foreigners on all occasions.
3. It is the business of Hollywood to shape the truth into box office contours.
4. What I am waiting for is a film about beautiful identical quintuplets who all love the same man.

WODEHOUSE, Pelham Grenville, born 1881
English humorous novelist.

1. The butler entered the room, a solemn procession of one.
2. The girl had as many curves as a scenic railway.
3. I could see that, if not actually disgruntled, he was far from being gruntled.
4. It was one of those parties where you cough twice before you speak and then decide not to say it after all.
5. She looked as if she had been poured into her clothes and had forgotten to say 'when'.
6. She turned him down like a bedspread.
7. Why don't you get a haircut; you look like a chrysanthemum.

WOODRUFF, Douglas, born 1897, *English essayist and editor.*

1. The great majority of the English move inside much too narrow an ambit of drinks, and many lives move between tea and beer.
2. Never ask a man how he made his first million.

3. Why be disagreeable, when with a little effort you can be impossible?

WOOLLCOTT, Alexander, 1887–1943
American journalist, dramatic critic, anthologist, author, and wit.

1. All the things I really like to do are either immoral, illegal, or fattening.
2. The audience strummed their catarrhs.
3. The English have an extraordinary ability for flying into a great calm.
4. Everything I know about her is merely daresay.
5. His huff arrived and he departed in it.
6. I must get out of these wet clothes and into a dry martini.
7. Many of us spend half our time wishing for things we could have if we didn't spend half our time wishing.
8. The scenery in the play was beautiful, but the actors got in front of it.
9. There's nothing wrong with Oscar Levant—nothing that a miracle couldn't cure.

WOTTON, Henry, 1568–1639, *English diplomat and poet.*

1. An ambassador is an honest man sent to lie abroad for the good of his country.
2. Hanging is the worst use man can be put to.
3. Next to no wife and children, your own wife and children are best pastime; another's wife and your children worse; your wife and another's children worst.
4. Tell the truth, and so puzzle and confound your adversaries.

WRIGHT, Thomas, 1810–1877, *English antiquary.*
Many kiss the child for love of the nurse.

WYCHERLEY, William, 1640?–1716, *English dramatist.*

1. Fi! madam, do you think me so ill-bred as to love a husband?
2. Go to your business, I say, pleasure, whilst I go to my pleasure, business.

3. He's a fool that marries; but he's a greater that does no
   marry a fool.
4. Next to the pleasure of making a new mistress is that o
   being rid of an old one.
5. She is as implacable an adversary as a wife suing fo
   alimony.

WYLIE, Philip, born 1902

American editor, columnist, and author.

We're about to enter the age of flight before we've eve developed a chair that a man can sit on comfortably.

WYNDHAM LEWIS, Denis Bevan, born 1884?

English humorist and biographer.

It is the proud perpetual boast of the Englishman that h never brags.

YBARRA, Thomas Russell, born 1880

American biographer and writer.

He owned and operated a ferocious temper.

YEATS-BROWN, Francis, 1886–1944

British army officer and author.

To me the charm of an encyclopedia is that it knows—and I needn't.

YOUNG, Edward, 1688–1765, *English poet.*

1. Scandal's the sweetener of a female feast.
2. What then is man? The smallest part of nothing.

ZANGWILL, Israel, 1864–1926, *English novelist and dramatist.*

1. Dead men hear no tales; posthumous fame is an Irish bull.
2. Editors are constantly on the watch to discover new talents in old names.
3. A man likes his wife to be just clever enough to comprehend his cleverness, and just stupid enough to admire it.
4. The only true love is love at first sight; second sight dispels it.
5. Scratch the Christian and you find the pagan—spoiled.

6. The way Bernard Shaw believes in himself is very refreshing in these atheistic days when so many believe in no God at all.

ZENO, *c.* 355, *Greek philosopher.*

1. Better to trip with the feet than with the tongue.
2. We have two ears and one mouth that we may listen the more and talk the less.

ZOLA, Émile, 1840–1902, *French novelist.*

1. If I cannot overwhelm with my quality, I will overwhelm with my quantity.
2. Perfection is such a nuisance that I often regret having cured myself of using tobacco.

Index

Index

All numbers in this index refer to quotations, not to pages. Since authors are arranged alphabetically in the dictionary, there is no need to give page numbers here.

Entries in this index generally consist of a key word, author's name, and quotation number. (ADVICE Billings, 10). This example indicates that the key word ADVICE is referred to in the tenth quotation under Billings.

When two or more authors have the same last name their initials are added to distinguish them (ADVICE J. Collins, 6).

When a key word or subject is followed by several authors these are separated by semicolons (ADVICE Bailey; Billings, 10; W. Churchill 1).

When an author is followed by numbers which are separated by commas these numbers refer to different quotations by him on the same subject (ADVICE Wilde, 89, 146).

When there is only one unnumbered quotation by an author in the dictionary, his name is not followed by any number in this index (ADVICE Bailey).